W9-BCA-386

The Painful Truth

Kathy felt she had to say *something* to try to save them both from total public humiliation. At last she cleared her throat and plunged ahead. "Listen, Deena, I don't know how to say this, but your ideas . . . well, they're too . . . what I mean is, they're so . . . I just don't think the kids are going to . . . "

"I don't need your advice, Kathy!" Deena's sharp tones resounded in the hall. "And I'm perfectly capable of handling this, thank you. Besides, even if the committee members are a bunch of reluctant recruits, they did elect me chairperson!"

Deena noticed her scattered papers and bent over to gather them up. "And now, if you'll excuse me, I'm already late!" She stood up again and marched off down the hall.

Cranberry Cousins
NO MORE PROMISES

BY CHRISTIE WELLS

A Troll Book

Acknowledgments

Many thanks to Lisa Eisenberg for her considerable creative contributions to this book.

Library of Congress Cataloging-in-Publication Data

Wells, Christie.
  No more promises / by Christie Wells.
     p.   cm.—(The Cranberry cousins; #4)
  Summary: Fifteen-year-old straight-A student Deena's struggle to
survive sharing a room with her outlandish cousin Kathy is
complicated by the sudden return of Deena's unreliable father, who
has had a history of breaking his promises since divorcing her
mother.
  ISBN 0-8167-1502-5 (lib. bdg.)   ISBN 0-8167-1503-3 (pbk.)
  [1. Cousins—Fiction. 2. Fathers and daughters—Fiction.]
I. Title. II. Series: Wells, Christie. Cranberry cousins; #4.
PZ7.W4635No 1989
[Fic]—dc19   88-16939

A TROLL BOOK, published by Troll Associates
Mahwah, NJ 07430

Copyright © 1989 by Troll Associates, Mahwah, New Jersey
All rights reserved. No part of this book may be used or
reproduced in any manner whatsoever without written
permission from the publisher.
Printed in the United States of America.
10 9 8 7 6 5 4 3 2 1

Chapter 1

"With a hey and a ho..." As Deena walked down the hallway at Cranford High, she sang a little song under her breath. "... and a hey nonny no ..." Outside it had been cloudy and gray all day long, but as Deena sang, a ray of sunshine suddenly beamed in through one of the high, narrow school windows and lit up the corridor in front of her. Perfect, Deena said to herself. Even the weather reflected her good mood.

She ran a hand over her neat, shoulder-length blond hair and hugged the thick pile of papers and folders she was clutching under one arm. Then she thought about all the reasons she had for being so happy. The main reason, of course, had to be the Spring Fling Entertainment Committee. The Spring Fling was *the* dance event of the year at Cranford High School. And not only was Deena on the entertainment committee, she was in *charge* of it. And if that wasn't an accomplishment for a new student

1

in school, then Deena didn't know the meaning of the word *accomplishment*!

She rounded the corner toward the multipurpose room and continued her mental review. Being on the committee, she realized, wasn't her only reason for feeling good. She felt good about Ken Buckly, too . . . or at least she *thought* she did.

Ken Buckly was a year ahead of her, a junior at Cranford, whom Deena had met through the ski club. He was smart, sweet, and unbelievably good-looking, and he and Deena were at the beginning stages of what Deena hoped would turn out to be a major romance. She was certainly crazy about *him*. But Ken was so popular and handsome and just plain incredible that she couldn't help worrying whether he could really truly be interested in her. He always seemed to have a million girls after him. Why, even her cousin Kathy had gone out with him for a while last winter. And Ken was the exact opposite of the punk type Kathy usually went for!

Still, there was no denying Ken had shown a little interest in Deena. Well, to be honest, more than just a little. He'd asked her out on several dates, and they'd had a fabulous time. At least Deena thought they had.

She sighed blissfully as she remembered the first time Ken had kissed her, and she felt her pulse quicken and her face grow hot. If only she could be sure he'd ask her out again! Particularly to the Spring Fling. She drifted off into a daydream and walked right into an open locker, painfully knocking her shoulder against the door. Deena shook her head; she had to stop fantasizing about Ken all the time. He was out of town for a week, at Concord, the state capital, serving as the school's representative in a government simulation game. So there was nothing she could do about Ken for the time being anyway. And besides, she'd always tried not to let boys become the number-one priority in her life.

She had lots of other reasons to be happy besides Ken Buckly, she thought. Her classes were stimulating, and she was getting all A's. And things were going well at home, too.

Deena thought some more about home and realized she was right. Contrary to all her expectations, the Cranberry Inn, the old restored Victorian inn run by her mother and aunt, was turning out to be a surprisingly pleasant place to live. In addition to that, though Deena's mother continued to put a lot of you-must-be-perfect pressure on her daughter, the two of them hadn't had a serious blowup in ages. And last, but certainly not least, Deena and her outrageous cousin Kathy had been getting along pretty well these days.

This was no small accomplishment in itself, Deena knew. For Kathy and Deena were totally opposite personalities. So it was almost comical that they were immediately lumped together as "The Cranberry Cousins"—after their moms' inn—for all eternity. But even nicknames had their advantages, Deena admitted, and virtually all of Cranford knew the cousins.

Although Deena and Kathy hadn't had a run-in in almost a month—a world's record—life wasn't a piece of cake by any means. Kathy was still an incredibly sloppy person with whom to share a room, and her taste in clothes and music went beyond all standards of . . .

3

At that instant, as if called forth by some kind of uncontrollable mental telepathy, Kathy stepped out of a nearby rest room and sauntered up the hall in Deena's direction. As usual, Kathy was a sight. She looked flagrantly flashy, with her freshly moussed spiky hair, dangling black feather earrings, and daringly short miniskirt. But still, Deena had to admit, her cousin looked pretty. Which, given Kathy's intensely freaky costume, was really saying something!

At that moment Kathy spotted her cousin. It was obvious from the way she skidded to a stop in her tracks that she was considering backing up into the rest room again. But then Deena saw her shrug her shoulders and keep on walking. Kathy probably realized she'd been spotted, Deena thought smiling to herself. And she knew she couldn't escape.

"Hi, Kathy!" she called down the hall. "Don't worry! It's late, and almost everyone has gone home for the day. There's very little chance of our being seen together."

Even from several yards away she saw a grin come onto Kathy's face. Deena felt pleased with herself. Kathy's sense of humor was so bizarre, it wasn't always easy to make her smile.

"Hi, Deena," Kathy said.

Deena came a few steps closer and peered intently at her cousin. "Are my eyes deceiving me," she asked, "or is your hair even more purple than usual?"

"It's not *purple* at all!" Kathy retorted. "I put on some warm raspberry highlights, that's all. You're only supposed to leave it on for thirty minutes, but I figured an hour would be a little more dramatic."

4

"If by 'dramatic' you mean more like a walking, talking pomegranate, then I guess you figured correctly!"

Kathy reached out for a lock of her cousin's hair. "You should really try some of this stuff," she said. "They have a shade called simmering saffron that would be a real sizzler on these blond tresses."

"It sounds delicious," Deena said laughing. "But we'll have to discuss it later. I have to hurry along now."

"Where are you going anyway? With all those papers, you look like you're on your way to a Future Bureaucrats of America Convention!"

Deena felt a familiar twinge of annoyance. Did Kathy have to make fun of *every* single thing she did? "For your information," she said out loud, "I'm on my way to a very important committee meeting. A committee, I might add, of which I am the chairperson!" Why'd I say it like that? Deena asked herself as soon as the words were out of her mouth. I sound like a conceited idiot!

Kathy made an elaborate sweeping bow, causing her short skirt to hike up another couple of inches. "Forgive me, Princess Dee! I had no idea I was in the presence of royalty. Please, please tell this lowly peasant what committee you're in charge of. The Chess Club Carnival? The Latin League Luncheon? The A-V Projectionists' Pic—"

"The Spring Fling Entertainment Committee!" Deena interrupted. She experienced a surge of triumph when she saw a spark of real interest flash into her cousin's newly made-up brown eyes. Kathy might pretend to sneer at programs sponsored by the school establishment, but she was passionate about anything and everything related to music and dancing.

"The Spring Fling Entertainment Committee?" Kathy repeated slowly. "I heard some pretty weird characters got roped into being on that one."

Deena looked thoughtful. "Well, now that you mention it, I was a bit surprised at the people who came to our first meeting last week. They didn't look like the type of volunteers I'd been expecting."

"They weren't. In fact, they weren't really volunteers at all. The Student Council couldn't find anyone to sign up for any of their committees this spring, so they cut a deal with Ms. Langton. Anyone who serves on an extracurricular committee this spring gets extra credit in civics. Something about learning to understand how the machinery of a community operates."

"Well, no one had to twist *my* arm to make me participate! I volunteered for the committee. I have a lot of ideas for upgrading the Spring Fling this year."

An anxious look crossed Kathy's face. Uh-oh, she was thinking. Here she goes again. Deena's planning some kind of big boring extravaganza.

"What exactly are these ideas of yours, Deena?" she asked cautiously.

"Well, I have so many, I hardly know where to begin. Almost anything we decide to do will be an improvement. According to my friend Tracy, last year they didn't even have a live band! They just stuck a boom box up on the stage and played tapes!"

"That does sound pretty feeble," Kathy admitted.

Deena was warming to her subject and didn't notice her cousin's dubious tones. "So that's why this spring I want to do something really incredible. I want to plan

6

a Spring Fling that's unlike any Spring Fling this school has ever seen before!"

"Such as?" Kathy asked. She was beginning to feel a little panicky, as she often did when Deena got carried away like this. Why couldn't her cousin ever do anything in a small way? Why did Deena always have to improve every single thing she touched?

Deena was so excited by her ideas, she didn't notice Kathy's expression. She began pawing through her massive multiple folders, dropping half of them onto her feet in the process. She was so enthusiastic, she wasn't even aware of the piles of papers spilling out and scattering themselves all over the floor.

"Listen to this one!" she said at last, triumphantly holding up a page full of notes. "I think it's really terrific. Just imagine this: a costume ball where everyone comes as a character from history. Then, for music, we have each person bring in a record or tape of authentic music from that time period!"

Kathy didn't say anything, but her frown deepened. This was even worse than she'd thought.

But Deena didn't seem to notice her silence. She unearthed another piece of paper and burbled on. "Or what about this idea? We decorate the gym to look like Bourbon Street in New Orleans, and then we stage a real-live Mardi Gras! We could play jazz music in the background and maybe even make some floats!"

"Deena . . . " Kathy tried to interrupt. But there was no stopping her cousin now.

"Or what about this idea, which I regard as my true *pièce de résistance*? In the gym we make an exact replica of one of those smoky basement nightclubs in Paris, you know, where those earthy people in the striped shirts hang out, and then we make a tape of *An American in Paris*, and—"

"*Deena!*" Kathy's voice was so loud it echoed up and down the corridor. Deena stopped chattering and stared in surprise.

"Deena," Kathy repeated more quietly. "Deena." Kathy couldn't think of what to say for a few seconds, which was almost unheard of for her. Normally she was never at a loss for a teasing or biting remark. But she knew exactly how her cousin handled criticism. She handled it terribly.

But Kathy felt she had to say *something* to try to save them both from total public humiliation. At last she cleared her thoughts and plunged ahead. "Listen, Deena, I don't know how to say this, but your ideas . . . well, they're too . . . what I mean is, they're so . . . I just don't think the kids are going to . . . "

"I don't need your advice, Kathy!" Deena's sharp tones resounded in the hall. "And I'm perfectly capable of handling this, thank you. Besides, even if the committee members are a bunch of reluctant recruits, they did elect me chairperson!"

Deena noticed her scattered papers and bent over to gather them up. "And now, if you'll excuse me, I'm already late!" She stood up again and marched off down the hall.

As Deena stomped along, she saw that the clouds had returned outside and completely blotted out the light that had been shining through the window a min-

8

ute before. How fitting, she told herself. Kathy had put her in a bad mood, and the weather knew it. Maybe I shouldn't have been so nasty just now. But truce or no truce, Kathy had really had it coming.

Deena tried to stop thinking about what Kathy had said, or tried to say, but it was no use. By the time she saw the door of the multipurpose room, most of her self-confidence had vanished with the sunshine. What if Kathy had been right? she wondered. What if there was something wrong with all of her ideas? If Kathy hadn't liked them, what were the other kids going to say?

But it was too late to do anything about that now. Deena had finally reached the multipurpose room and could hear the sound of raised voices coming from within. She pulled open the door and stepped inside to face the other members of her committee.

Chapter 2

D eena wasn't the only one who was feeling worried. As Kathy hurried out of the school yard, she ordered her brain to shut up and get out of town. But she just couldn't stop worrying. Maybe she should have asked Deena to take her along to that meeting. From what she'd heard of who was on that committee, no one else would have a single idea about the theme for the dance. Which meant that Deena would be able to railroad through one of her crazy ideas without anybody lifting a finger to stop her. Which meant the Spring Fling would be some kind of uplifting, intellectual experience that everyone at school would loathe—and Kathy would be blamed because she was Deena's cousin and hadn't done anything to stop her!

But what could she have done? she thought as she cut through the parking lot. Deena didn't want to hear what she had to say, she had made that perfectly clear, and . . .

Her thoughts were cut short by the sound of a loud, piercing wolf whistle. "Yo, babeee!" shouted a male voice. "Looking good today, sugar!"

Kathy didn't even turn her head. She knew who was shouting, and she didn't want to look at him. It was Danny Lardner—or "Ace," as he liked to be called, the gleetch of Cranford. He'd been kicked out of school a few years ago for trashing the cafeteria, and he'd never bothered to re-enroll. Now he just hung around town harassing people, particularly girls at the high school. He was bad news. Even Kathy's friend Zee wouldn't have anything to do with him, and she'd hang out with almost *anybody*!

Kathy quickened her pace, leaving Ace Lardner behind. Once again she started worrying about Deena and her dance plans. Oh, knock it off! she told herself. What else could she have done? There was no reasoning with Deena when she was on a roll. Besides, Kathy hadn't wanted to hang around school. Today she had a really good reason for getting home early!

As she turned up the front walk to the inn, she saw the reason, perched high up on a ladder on the south side of the building, and her heart went into its usual beat-skipping routine. It was Kathy's boyfriend, Roy Harris. He'd taken a part-time job with a bunch of painters, who were painting the Cranberry Inn's exterior. It was going to use up most of his free time for the next month or so, which was a real bummer. But, on the other hand, he'd be working right under her nose, so at least she'd be able to keep an eye on him. And besides that, Roy was earning the extra money so he could buy a radical new motorcycle. Kathy hoped she'd be glued to the seat behind him when he took it out for its first fantastic ride.

She hurried around the corner of the house and stood at the bottom of the ladder. "Hey, Roy!" she called up. "Do you want to come down and . . . "

RrrrrRRRRRRR! Kathy's words were blasted away by a tremendous explosion of sound. All at once a half pound of sand fell directly into her open mouth. "Gross!" As she gagged and spat the sand out onto the ground, the roaring sound suddenly stopped.

"Hey, Roy! What's the big idea?"

The boy on the ladder twisted around to peer down at her. He was wearing thick plastic goggles and some kind of enormous gas mask. He looked like an alien invader. "Who . . . ?" he said. "Oh, hi there, Manelli! I didn't see you down there."

"Well, I'm here! What's the big idea of throwing sand on me?"

Roy acted as if he hadn't heard her. He brushed a lock of his thick dark hair away from his forehead. "Listen, Manelli!" he shouted down at her. "You'd better get out of here. They're sandblasting the paint off the chimney over here, and the sand is flying all over the place."

"Now you tell me," Kathy muttered. But once again her words were lost in the thunder of the sandblaster. As a second load of sand sprayed up into the air and began falling on her head, she turned on her heels and ran back around the corner.

Well, so much for hanging out with Roy after school today, she told herself as she brushed the sand out of her

12

hair onto the inn porch. As long as he was tied up with that sandblaster, she was out of there!

She went in the front door, hauled off her shiny orange and black satin Bowl-a-Rama jacket, and tossed it onto the nearest chair. Another load of sand slid off the jacket's slick, slippery shoulders and made two tiny twin side-by-side sand dunes on the floor.

"Oops." Kathy scowled at the sand piles. She supposed she *should* go get a dustpan and brush from the kitchen and sweep up the stuff. But it would be a real drag, and besides, was it worth it? After all, she reasoned, with all that sand flying around outside, guests will be tracking it in all day. The hall will just get messed up again. So why bother cleaning it up now? She could do it later. Or better yet, maybe someone else would do it later!

With that question settled to her satisfaction, she went on to the next problem. What *was* she going to do right now? She'd only been home half a minute, and she was already bored. She was also disappointed. Roy had been so busy with his after-school odd-job business, she felt as if she hadn't seen him for days. Lately she'd begun to wonder if they were still really even going together at all. When he'd told her about the job at the inn, she'd thought she might have a chance to see a bit more of him. But not if she had to compete with the sandblaster for his attention!

Sadly Kathy thought about the fun she and Roy had had riding around on his motorcycle last fall before Roy had become so hardworking. Maybe later, she thought hopefully, when he gets off work, he'll have some time for a ride. But in the meantime there was no reason in the world for her to be hanging around this yawn factory!

As she picked a grain of sand out of her teeth, she realized she was hungry for some real food. She decided to have a snack and then call some of her friends, like Zee or Ellecia, to see if one of them wanted to do something. She wandered through the dining room, where she gave a vague nod to an elderly inn guest who was sitting at one of the gleaming cherry tables, sketching the view out the window.

In the kitchen she found her little brother, Johnny, pawing through the open refrigerator.

"Anything decent to eat in there, brat?" she asked him affectionately as she pulled upon the pantry door.

"Not unless you think bean sprouts are decent!" he answered, slamming the refrigerator with a bang. "Mom's trying to kill us."

Kathy stared dejectedly at a bag of unsweetened bran nuggets and a box of soy-protein wafers on the cupboard shelf. "I know what you mean," she nodded. "In California she always used to stock some basic junk food in the house. But ever since she unpacked that weird sixties book on holistic cooking by that Indian guru . . . "

"Starvation City," Johnny said mournfully.

Kathy handed him a soy wafer. He took one bite and threw the rest in the garbage. Muttering darkly about dried-up cardboard, he stomped out of the kitchen. He looked so depressed, Kathy couldn't help laughing at him. Then she spied a bag of apples on the counter. They were not Twinkies, she said to herself, but they would have to do. She helped herself to a big juicy one and bit into it. Chewing noisily, she went to the parlor phone and settled into an antique chair to make some calls.

Six conversations later she gave up in disgust. Three kids weren't home, two were already busy, and one was actually doing her homework. A new idea dawned on Kathy, and she stopped chewing for a minute to consider it.

She could do *her* homework, she supposed, absent-mindedly scratching a nailful of sand out of her hair. But she was saved from having to think about that idea any longer when she spotted something else on the hall table.

It was a stack of sheet music she'd put on the table when she'd come home three days ago. She'd been given the music by Mike Iwasaki, who was a radically punk junior from school. Mike was an extremist in every way—politically and personally, with the wildest, fuzziest, most airborne hair Kathy had ever seen. He was also a really superhot electric guitarist. He was the leader of a struggling band called Dementia.

"I heard you sing in the school musical, Kathy," he'd told her last week. "It goes without saying that the songs were pretty cutsie-pie. But your voice was something else . . . really out of sight. I think that if you and I got together, we'd be able to make some great music. Plus I know the guys on Dementia would really get their act together if I could deliver a good lead singer."

Kathy had liked the compliment, so she'd taken Mike's music and told him she was interested in singing

15

with Dementia sometime soon. But in her heart she'd had a lot of doubts. For sure, she'd loved singing with the band back home in San Francisco, and she'd thought she'd love singing with a band here. But so far Kathy hadn't felt ready.

She leaned back in the chair and thought about Fury, the one garage band she had sung with in Cranford. She'd sung some with them. Those guys were O.K.— they were good musicians and all. But it just hadn't felt like family, the way the band back home used to.

She peeled a few sheets of music off the pile and stared down at the top song. She recognized it right away. "Break My Chains." She'd never performed it herself, but it had been a big hit for the Tortured Tailpipes, another group from her school in San Francisco.

She studied the first few notes of "Break My Chains," then tried to sing them out loud. Not bad, she told herself. Except for that one high note. Just then she remembered the old piano in the front parlor.

It was probably totally out of tune, she thought as she got to her feet and went to the parlor door. But it was better than nothing. And it beat homework by a mile.

She walked into the parlor and propped up the sheet music on the piano. She started singing again, and soon realized how out of practice she was. She sat down on the piano bench and started to pick out the melody on the smooth white keys. After a minute her voice warmed up, and she belted out the song as if she'd been singing it all her life. Sounding good, Manelli! she told herself. Maybe she *would*

16

call Mike Iwasaki and ask if she could practice with Dementia this week. She smiled and turned to the next song in the pile, "Brother, Can You Spare Some Slime?"

She started to play the melody, but stopped after the first few notes. Some fine, white grainy stuff was drifting down from the ceiling and landing on the piano keys. At first Kathy thought the sand from the sandblaster was somehow spraying in through an open window. But all the windows in the parlor were closed, and the noise from outside had temporarily stopped, so that had to mean the machine wasn't even running.

In a few seconds the white grains stopped falling, and Kathy started to play again. But before she'd gotten through two bars, a big flake of plaster plunked down and smacked her right on the top of her nose. "What's going on here?" she yelled. "First I get sand in my mouth, and now I'm getting plaster in my face, just when I was starting to enjoy myself!" Angrily she slammed down the cover over the keyboard and stalked out of the room to investigate.

Upstairs, Kathy headed for the nearest of the two rooms that were directly over the front parlor. She pounded loudly on the first door, but no one answered, and after a minute she decided the room was empty. She moved toward the back of the building and drummed on the second guest room door. Again no one responded. But this time Kathy heard banging and pounding coming from inside the room.

17

"What's going on here?" she asked again. She opened the door and stepped into the room. Then she stopped and stood stock still. "Aunt Lydia!" she said. "What on earth are you doing?"

Lydia turned around to look at her niece, and Kathy's mouth dropped open in surprise. Aunt Lydia was usually the most stylish, best-groomed, *tidiest* person in the cosmos. But right now she looked like a wild woman. Her normally neat frosted hair was standing out around her face like a lion's mane. Her shirt and slacks were covered with powdery white plaster. Her arms and hands were filthy. But the strangest and most scary thing was her face. Aunt Lydia's usually polite, proper expression had vanished. Now her cheeks were flushed from exertion, and her eyes were glowing with enthusiasm.

"Come over here, Kathy!" she ordered.

Kathy took one reluctant step. If Aunt Lydia had snapped her twig, it probably wasn't a good idea to get too close to her. After all, how well did she really know Aunt Lydia anyway? And wasn't it always controlled, well-organized people who finally totally shorted out their circuits?

"What are you waiting for?" her aunt demanded. "Come over here!"

Kathy took one more step. Then she saw what her aunt was holding in her dirty hands. A long, black, heavy, lethal-looking metal weapon! That does it, Kathy thought. Out loud, she said, "Aunt Lydia, I'm not taking another step till you tell me what you're doing with that crowbar!"

Aunt Lydia stared at her, and then a smile appeared on her smudged face. "I'm sorry, Kathy," she said. "I guess I'm getting a little carried away here. I told everyone about my new project at dinner last night. I forgot you were having pizza with your friend Ellecia."

"So what is your new project?"

Aunt Lydia put down her crowbar and gestured around the room. "This," she said. "This room. It's too small to use as a guest room, so I'm converting it into a reading room—a sort of second-story library."

"You need a crowbar for that? Can't you just stick some bookshelves and a chair in here?"

Lydia laughed. "Actually, my first idea was to do just that. But then last night I was cleaning out a closet, and I found some of the original plans for the inn tucked away in an old box. According to the blueprints, the architect intended for this room to have a fireplace. Now it seemed to me that a fireplace would be absolutely perfect for a reading room, but I wasn't certain whether the fireplace had ever been built, or whether some past owner had plastered it over for some reason, so..."

"So you're bashing the wall with a crowbar to find out?"

"More or less," said Lydia. "When I knocked on this portion of the wall, it definitely had a different sound to it, and since the plaster was peeling off anyway, I decided I might as well take a look behind it. And now I think I see something very interesting back here. If you could just come over here and help me remove this one piece, it would be an enormous help."

Uh-oh, thought Kathy. Disaster ahead. Once Aunt Lydia dragged you into a project, you could never claw your way out again.

"I don't know, Aunt Lydia," she said, desperately trying to come up with a plausible excuse for leaving. "I'm really busy doing my homework, and . . ."

RRRRRrrrrr! For the third time that afternoon, she was interrupted by the now familiar roar of the sandblaster starting up again. As usual, it was deafeningly loud. But this time there was also something intriguing about the noise. It sounded as if it were right outside!

Kathy crossed the room to the window and looked out. Then she caught her breath and grinned. Roy's heavily goggled, masked face was only a few inches away from her own. The chimney he was working on *was* right outside the room.

After a minute Roy noticed Kathy's face at the window. When he saw her, he winked behind his goggles—or at least she *thought* he did—and once again her heart thudded in her rib cage. Even in his ugly mask Roy looked terrific. And he was obviously happy to see her.

Oh, well. It wasn't exactly a date, but it was better than nothing. Kathy pressed her face up against the window and winked back at Roy. Then she turned around to face her aunt. "I guess I don't mind hanging around in here for a while, Aunt Lydia," she said. "What do you want me to do?"

Chapter 3

Deena left the school grounds slowly, barely noticing the threatening black clouds gathering over her head. Even when the wind picked up speed and the temperature began to drop, she still strode along, lost in her thoughts. As she cut through the parking lot, she didn't even hear the sound of the motorcycle until it was only a few feet away. Finally, though, she realized someone was actually speaking to her.

"Hey, there, Blondie. It looks like rain. Why don't you hop on here with me and I'll save you from the showers?"

Startled, Deena looked up, right into Ace Lardner's stubby, leering face. Then she glanced behind him at the empty parking lot. For some reason the gang of louts that sometimes accompanied Ace was nowhere to be seen. And neither was anyone else.

Deena wished the town of Cranford would do something about this person hanging around outside the school all the time. It was like running the gauntlet every afternoon just to get past him!

Out loud she cleared her throat and said primly, "No thank you, Ace. I prefer to walk."

For some reason this remark made Ace laugh out loud. "O.K., Blondie," he said as he gunned his engine and rode off. "But anytime you want to take me up on the offer, I'll be available!"

As Ace roared away, a huge raindrop plopped down and struck Deena right on the forehead. She lifted her face to the sky. "Oh, go ahead and rain if you feel like it!" she said to the dreary clouds. "You couldn't put me in a worse mood if you tried."

More drops fell, and the wind became even more brisk. Deena wished she'd remembered to bring a sweater to school. But that morning the weather had been so warm, she hadn't thought it would be necessary.

Everything had looked better this morning, she thought ruefully. Before that horrendous committee meeting!

She was desperately trying not to dwell on the meeting anymore, but she wasn't having much luck. She just couldn't prevent herself from rehashing the last thirty minutes over and over in her mind. What had happened? Where had she gone wrong? How could something that had started out so happily manage to transform itself into such a living nightmare?

She didn't have to look very far for the answer. Without a doubt, she concluded, it had been entirely the fault of that horrible friend of Kathy's, Zee. Deena had never forgiven Zee for the time she'd put pizza on Deena's seat in front of a whole group of kids in a restaurant. It had been a mean, nasty, childish thing to do. And it had been right in character.

Looking back on the meeting now, Deena realized that Zee had been on some kind of power trip and had probably wanted to chair the committee herself. So when the other kids had voted for Deena, Zee must have decided to sabotage any and all of Deena's suggestions.

It wasn't that Deena couldn't handle a little constructive criticism, she told herself. But Zee traveled far beyond constructive, into the world of just plain mean. And it was pretty clear she was enjoying herself. From the very beginning of the meeting, she was on the attack.

Deena relived the whole meeting in vivid Technicolor. In her mind's eye she saw herself going into the multipurpose room and innocently putting her pile of folders on the table. Before she even had a chance to sit down, Zee said, "Like, wow. Like, I think I might just have a heart attack because I am *so* excited about seeing some more ideas from the human paper factory."

Deena had flushed but maintained her self-control. "Well, yes, I *have* come up with some more ideas," she said. "Though I don't want to foist them on anyone who doesn't like them. Do any of you have any other suggestions to make?"

As she glanced around the table at the silent, staring committee members, she began to feel really worried. How on earth, she asked herself, had the Student Council ever come up with such a stupid idea as giving extra credit in civics for being on a school committee? It was a perfect way of guaranteeing you'd get a bunch of apathetic, bored clods who didn't give a hoot about their project. And this quirky cast of characters certainly proved her point!

Take the person at her immediate right, for instance. Steve Rutherford, known by one and all as Steve Ruthernerd. Even as Deena gazed at his pale, skinny face, he was so intently absorbed with his ever-present, much-beloved slide rule, he didn't bother to look up. What did he know or care about the theme for the Spring Fling? Steven's idea of entertainment was solving a page full of quadratic equations!

And it didn't get any better after Steve. Next to him sat—or rather slumped—the round, sleeping form of Zack Rollins, whose only claim to fame was the cafeteria record for devouring the most ice-cream sandwiches in one lunch period—followed by the loudest recorded belch in school history. Beside Zack was Sally Brown, sometimes known as "Irongirl" for her single-minded devotion to every kind of athletics known to New England. Next to Sally was Rainier Helmutte, the Finnish exchange student, who hadn't learned a single word of English in his eight months at Cranford High, and who, as a consequence, never even opened his mouth.

Blond, witchy-haired Zee sat next to Rainier, and next to Zee was cute, curly-haired Trish Boswell, the school airhead. Trish opened her mouth to speak, but Zee cut her off before she had a chance to say anything.

"News flash! News flash from outer space!" she said. "I'm tuning in a message on my extraterrestrial sonar antenna!" She pointed a long, purple-painted fingernail at

24

Deena, and her dangling, coffin-shaped earring slapped against the side of her neck. Then she started speaking in the mechanical voice of a robot. "Here is the mes-sage. Your ideas from last week were so barfy they make all earth people want to puke."

Deena swallowed hard and looked around at the other members, hoping for some kind of support. But all she saw were amused faces. "Well," she admitted, "perhaps some of my ideas were a bit elaborate . . . "

"That's what I think!" Trish burst out in her high, breathless voice. "They were sweet ideas, of course, Deena, but they'd take so much work! I think we should have the kind of Spring Fling they've always had before. You know, with some tapes of . . . I don't know, maybe the Bubble Gums or something . . . and dancing, of course . . . and . . . I know! Some really yummy punch!"

A long pause followed. "And that's it?" Deena finally asked in disappointment. "That's all you really want?"

"Well, I suppose we could tape some fake paper flowers on the basketball backboards and spray some perfume on them if you think we should have decorations."

Deena worked hard to make her voice sound normal. "I was hoping, Trish," she said, raising her voice to be heard over the sound of Zack Rollins's snoring, "that we might do something a little different this year. Now maybe my ideas aren't perfect, but I'm sure if we put our heads together . . . "

As she spoke, she distinctly heard a loud piggy "Oink!" coming from Zee's direction. Deena pretended not to hear, but everyone else certainly did. Even Steve glanced up from his slide rule to see what was going on.

25

After that the progress of the meeting was straight downhill, with Sally flipping through a sporting goods catalogue, Zack snoring louder and louder, Rainier staring at the wall, and Steve scribbling calculations on his poorly fitted shirtsleeve. Trish politely but stubbornly continued to gush over her mundane idea about Bubble Gum tapes and some punch, and Zee made a multitude of sarcastic jokes at Deena's expense. By the time they adjourned, Deena was reduced to a jumpy, irritable, anxious bundle of nerves.

Worse yet, she didn't have anyone to discuss the problem with. Her best friend, Pat, was visiting her grandparents in Key West. And Ken, whom she sometimes talked to, was away in Concord. And anyway, she thought now, coming back to the present as she came within sight of the inn, it was probably just as well Ken *was* out of town! She would have died of embarrassment if he heard how that creepy Zee had made a fool out of her. How *could* Kathy be friends with such a person? And how could *Deena* save the Spring Fling from being an utter disaster? If she went along with Trish—who was the only person on the committee besides Zee who'd even opened her mouth—the Spring Fling would be boring and stupid, and Deena would feel like a failure. But if she couldn't come up with a better idea that everyone would accept, what else could she do?

As she turned up the walk to the inn, there was a loud clap of thunder, and torrents of rain began pouring from the sky. Deena sprinted toward the building, almost colliding with a group of workmen who were hurrying to seek shelter on the front porch. She thought she recognized Roy, Kathy's boyfriend, although it was difficult to be sure because he was wearing some kind of face mask. It was probably some new kind of punk costume, she decided, like the Band-Aid box earring he'd worn on his ear for a few weeks last winter. She wondered what he was doing outside in the rain instead of hanging around inside with Kathy as he usually did, listening to punk music and helping himself to record-breaking amounts of food.

She went inside and put her soggy papers down to dry out on a chair in the hall. As she did, she accidentally knocked over two small piles of sand on the floor. The sand immediately stuck to the bottoms of her wet shoes. Her footsteps made a gritty, scrunching sound as she stalked into the kitchen for a dustpan and brush.

Sweeping up the sand made Deena's bad mood even worse. That Johnny, she thought as she crawled along the floor with the brush, following her grainy trail. She loved that boy, but Aunt Nancy was as easygoing with him as she was with Kathy. She let him get away with murder around here. He had to learn to clean up after himself!

After she finished sweeping, Deena went upstairs to do her homework, as she always did. But today she just couldn't concentrate. For one thing she couldn't put that terrible committee meeting out of her mind. But the main distraction was that Kathy's half of the room resembled a federal disaster area even more than it usually did— which was really saying something.

Deena gazed around the room, trying to figure out what had changed. "Aha!" Her eyes grew wide as she realized what was happening. Kathy's mess was *growing*—spreading like some kind of destructive monstrous slime in a horror movie! Her dense, three-foot-deep chaotic clutter was definitely taking up at least two-thirds—maybe even three-quarters!—of the room.

"If this is allowed to go on, in a week I'll be trapped in here with no air to breathe!" Deena cried. "I'll be smothered alive! They'll find my body in next spring's thaw!"

In a sudden frenzy she jumped to her feet and started grabbing up Kathy's shoes, scarves, vests, hats, books, make-up, homework, school notices, posters, magazines, letters from California, sweaters, skirts, socks, boots, leg warmers, tape player, brush, comb, hair dryer, candy wrappers, gum wrappers, and empty soda cans and hurling them onto her cousin's unmade bed. She wished she had a pitchfork as she whirled around the room, snatching and tossing. It probably wasn't safe to touch some of these things with her bare hands. Heaven only knew what Kathy had buried under there!

As she cleaned up, she yanked Kathy's favorite U.C.L.A. nightshirt from the top of a lamp, and several cassettes fell out of the sleeve and clattered onto the floor. Deena grabbed them up, too, and was about to pitch them onto the pile on the bed when she caught sight of one of the labels.

"The Bubble Gums," she read out loud. That was the group Trish Boswell wanted to use for the Spring Fling. It was odd that Kathy would have a cassette of the group's music. A band with a name like that could never produce a weird enough sound for Kathy's tastes. Probably the cassette had been a loan from one of Kathy's less far-out friends who hadn't realized that lending something to Kathy was the same thing as hurling it into a deep, black pit.

Still holding the Bubble Gums cassette in her hand, Deena slowly sat down on the tiny open space that remained on top of her cousin's bed. Kathy, Kathy, Kathy, she thought. She might be a messy pig, but she did know a lot about music and dancing. She had a strange way of thinking, but she did have her moments of intelligence, and a lot of kids at school really respected her ideas. She just might be the perfect person to help brainstorm a good theme for the Spring Fling.

Quickly Deena got to her feet. Then, just as quickly, she plopped back down again, dislodging her newly made pile of Kathy's belongings. The heap fell off the bed and spread itself out on the floor again, as if it had never been touched. Deena barely noticed.

She *couldn't* talk to Kathy about this. She'd already jumped down her cousin's throat this afternoon, saying she was perfectly capable of handling this. If she went to Kathy for advice now, Kathy'd probably laugh in Deena's face!

She sighed and sat quietly for a minute. Then a new thought came to her. What about her mother? She didn't know a thing about music, but she did have a level head on her shoulders. Lydia would understand about Deena's high standards—she'd been the one who always insisted on them! Besides, mothers were always asking to know what went on in school. They adored being asked for advice. Just because Deena had never gotten herself into any kind of trouble in the past, it didn't mean she couldn't ask for help now.

Once again she got to her feet and kicked a path through Kathy's things toward the door. As she left her room, she realized she was already feeling cheerier at the idea of talking to her mother. What she needed was a clear-headed, rational approach to this dumb problem. And Mom was rational to a fault. Who knew that better than her own daughter?

She went downstairs to the kitchen, expecting to find Lydia in her usual place, efficiently bustling around supervising dinner preparations. But instead, she found only her cousin Johnny. He was busily stirring a pot full of goo on top of the stove.

"Johnny!" she said. "You know you're not allowed to use the stove without an adult in the room. And that flame is way too high. What on earth are you making, anyway?"

"Marshmallows."

"You're *making* marshmallows?"

"Well, not exactly," Johnny explained. "See, I found this old bag of them in the cupboard. I think they're left over from last summer, and . . . "

"If they're left over from last summer, that makes them nearly a year old, Johnny!"

"I know. That's probably why they're hard as rocks. So anyway, I thought if I heated them up a little and threw in some peanut butter—"

"Enough!" Deena exclaimed. "You're making me

sick. Just tell me where my mother is so I can get out of here."

Johnny shrugged. "I don't know where she is. Do you think this stuff would taste good on a hot dog roll? I saw some in the freezer."

"No! What do you mean, you don't know where my mother is? She's supposed to be in charge of you during the afternoons Aunt Nancy goes to pottery class."

"Oh, she's around somewhere I think. Here. Taste this. Maybe it needs some jelly." He scraped some glop from the bottom of his smoking pan and waved it in Deena's direction. She took one look at the slimy concoction on the spoon, gagged, and ran out of the kitchen.

She went through the rooms on the first floor, checking for her mother in each one. This was really getting odd, she thought as she headed for the stairs. She wondered if mom could have forgotten about Johnny and gone out somewhere!

But *someone* else was home. As she walked down the hallway on the second floor, she was positive something was going on in one of the empty guest rooms. She heard some kind of unidentified scratching and scraping noises. Then she heard the sound of her mother's voice, talking to someone and laughing.

Aunt Nancy must have cut pottery, she thought. Who else could be in there with mom?

She knocked softly, but there was no answer. She turned the knob and pushed open the door. She started to go in, but then she stopped to stare.

The scene inside the room was surprising, to say the

least. Deena's mother and *Kathy*—of all people!—were sitting side by side near a gaping hole in the far wall. Their hair, faces, and clothes were covered with a fine, white, powdery dust. Lydia had her arm around Kathy's shoulders, and they were both gazing intently at something inside the hole. The two of them were chattering and squealing like a pair of second graders!

"Mom?" Deena called from the doorway.

Lydia didn't even hear her. "Just look at the detail on that one, Kathy!" she exclaimed. "I'm sure it's hand-painted."

"Those little kids look really real," Kathy said. "Are they supposed to be dancing, or what?"

"*Mom?*"

Again Lydia didn't turn around. She picked up a tool and scraped something on the wall. "They seem to be standing in a circle of some kind," she said as she worked. "Why, Kathy! I believe they're playing ring-around-a-rosy!"

"No kidding! I think you're right. Wow, that's really—"

"MOM!" Deena's call from the doorway was almost a shout. Both Kathy and Lydia jumped. Then they turned around and gaped at her as if she'd lost her mind. "For heaven's sake, Deena," her mother said sharply. "Why are you screaming at me like that?"

"I . . . I just wanted to let you know I'm home, and I wanted to talk to you about—"

"Wait until you see what we've uncovered here, dear!" Lydia broke in. "You remember I told you I was going to convert this room into a reading room?"

"I guess so, but now I—"

32

"Well, Kathy and I have been slaving away in here, and we just discovered the most amazing fireplace tiles behind all this plaster!"

"I can't believe anyone ever plastered them up like this," Kathy added. "I wonder if there's a dead body back here or something."

Lydia laughed. "I guess we'll find out eventually," she said. "Though we certainly have a lot more plaster to chip away." She suddenly seemed to recall Deena, standing on the far side of the room. "Come on in here, Deena," she called. "You can help us. It's fascinating work. Like being a detective."

Deena stared at the powdery dust and chips of plaster that covered the floor. She didn't know why, but she was sure she didn't want to get involved in uncovering the tiles. It wasn't just the mess, which wasn't even as extreme as Kathy's half of the bedroom. It was more that she had the distinct impression she was interrupting—and that her mother didn't particularly care whether Deena joined in the project or not. "No thanks, Mom," she said. "I haven't finished my homework yet."

"Fine, dear," her mother called. "But before you get too involved in your work, would you mind preheating the oven for the guests' stuffed capons? I gave Mrs. Wiggins a few days off to visit her daughter, so we'll have to manage on our own in the kitchen. There are only a few guests, so it shouldn't be too bad, but I've been so absorbed up here, I just haven't had a chance to think about food."

Deena started to answer, but she stopped when she realized her mother's head was already deep inside the hole in the wall again. Wonderful, she said to herself as she went back downstairs. Her committee had turned on her, the boy she liked was out of town and hadn't even called, and now her mother was so busy chipping plaster she couldn't even spare the time to talk to her!

She headed through the dining room and wrinkled her nose in disgust. Now this is all I need, she thought when she saw the state of the kitchen. To top everything off, her other cousin had filled the house with stinky smoke, spilled boiled marshmallows and peanut butter all over the top of the stove, and left a charred, smelly potful of blackened glue soaking in the sink. If the guests got a whiff of that, they'd be heading for the Inn of the Flying Goose over in Middleville for sure!

She opened the kitchen window to air out the smoke, and another fat raindrop flew inside and hit her square in the face. Well, that was just perfect. The perfect end for a perfectly *horrible* day!

Chapter 4

Two days later Deena sat at her desk doing her home-work, feeling in a much better mood. She wasn't sure why she felt so much happier. She still had all her problems: she still hadn't come up with an idea for the Spring Fling theme, Lydia still hadn't found the time for a talk, Ken was still out of town and still hadn't gotten around to calling yet, and Kathy's unsightly accumulation of mess was still oozing all over Deena's half of the room.

But nonetheless, Deena felt good. Her naturally cheerful spirits just wouldn't stay down. After watching a public television documentary on a drought in East Africa last night, she'd realized her problems just weren't that big a deal. Given time, she was sure she'd find solutions for all of them. Besides, who could be depressed on a wonderful Saturday spring morning like this? The sun was shining, the birds were singing, and a warm breeze was blowing in the window. Also, there was nothing like writing to Whitney Stanton, one of her best friends from Boston, while listening to opera on a good pair of headphones to help a person forget her troubles.

She turned up the volume on her stereo and hummed a few bars of *La Bohème* in harmony with Luciano Pavarotti. She was warbling like a lark when the door suddenly burst open, and Kathy charged into the room. "Deena!" she yelled. "What's the matter? Should I dial nine—one—one or the ASPCA?"

Deena's light mood immediately became a few shades darker. Why did Kathy always *do* this to her? She pulled her headphones off her ears to answer. "I was singing," she said shortly.

Kathy let out her breath in a long, exaggerated sigh. "Oh, what a relief!" she said. "I thought I heard a cat being strangled to death in here!"

Deena put her headphones back on top of her head and sneered. "You make remarks like that," she said in an overly loud voice, "because you don't appreciate decent music. You only like sounds created by slamming garbage can lids together."

"Hey!" Kathy said. "Garbage can lids. That's not a bad idea. I did some singing with Mike Iwasaki and Dementia yesterday, and maybe they'd be interested in a new sound like . . ."

She stopped talking when she realized Deena couldn't hear her because of her headphones. But thinking about garbage can lids had given her a sudden urge to listen to Felix Freakout's latest album, *Rockin' Rotten*. She pawed through the jumbled piles of cassettes on her desk, floor, and chair, but couldn't find Felix anywhere. At last she tried feeling the floor under her bed. Jackpot! Her searching fingers pulled out not only Felix, but also her missing yellow sneaker and a dusty but unopened pack of gum.

What a find! In one easy motion Kathy popped a piece of gum in her mouth and snapped Felix Freakout into her cassette player. She reached for her headphones, but then glanced at Deena and changed her mind. She and Deena didn't *both* need to wear phones at one time, she thought. And besides, she couldn't dance around very well with hers on.

She pressed *play* and waited for the music to start. But when Felix started singing "Eat My Toenails," she could barely even hear the beat of the synthesizer. She adjusted the controls on each speaker, but then the background music started drowning out Felix's voice. The only answer, obviously, was to turn up the volume one full twist of the knob. Maybe another half a twist would be better. One more full twist. Ahhh. Perfection. If only Dementia could play like that, she'd promise to be their lead singer for the rest of her life!

Kathy picked up her hair dryer and started lip-synching words into it, pretending she was singing into a microphone as she danced to the beat. By the time the singer started in on the second song, "Sludge," she was really into the music. For a few minutes Kathy Manelli *was* Felix Freakout in the flesh.

Deena, on the other hand, was staring at her cousin in wide-eyed astonishment. This had to be seen to be believed. No, she said to herself. No, Kathy wasn't having a fit. She hadn't been possessed by Satan. She was doing this on purpose!

It simply *had* to be intentional! Anyone—even Kathy—had to be aware that her music was playing so loud it was shaking the very foundations of an inn that had stood, firmly anchored on this ground, for close to two centuries. There was no question about it. Kathy was trying to drive her crazy! "She probably thinks," Deena muttered out loud, "that with me locked up, she can have the whole room to herself. That way she can cover the *whole* floor with her stuff!"

Well, Deena had put up with a lot from her cousin, but this was the last straw. She wasn't taking this sitting down!

She got to her feet, yanked her headphones' cord from the side of her stereo, and turned *La Bohème* up to full volume. "*Amor, amor a*-MOOOOOR!" screamed Mimi and Rodolfo. "Sludge, sludge, SLUDGE!" squawled Felix Freakout.

The deafening din was so loud, Deena wanted to cover her ears and run out of the room. But she wasn't leaving until she'd tasted the fruits of her revenge. She wanted to see Kathy down on the floor, begging Deena to turn down the volume on her opera.

But something was going wrong with her plan. Instead of falling to her knees, crying for mercy, Kathy was still writhing around the room, making the frenzied movements she thought of as "dancing." For some reason she was yelling into her hair dryer. And the expression on her face was ecstatic!

I give up, Deena decided after a moment. I can't take it anymore. I cry uncle. She wins. She went to her stereo and snapped the control to Off. Marcello abruptly stopped bellowing about pretty ladies, and Felix Freakout's grunts were the only sound left in the room.

She was about to go over and turn down the volume on Kathy's cassette player when her cousin suddenly stopped dancing and frowned. "Say, Deena," she said. "Don't turn that off. It sounded great with Felix. I was trying to figure out a way we could mix the two sounds together and make a tape of it."

Deena stared at her cousin in astonishment. Then she laughed out loud. Only Kathy could think the greatest opera singers in the world should sing back-up for Felix Freakout! Her cousin might be a real pain in the neck, but she was certainly one of a kind.

A new thought came to her. "What are you doing in here, Kathy?" she yelled over the opening yowls of Felix's next song. "I thought you and my mother were still restoring the fireplace in the reading room!"

"We are!" Kathy shouted back. "But we had to stop because your mom went to the store for some new kind of cleaning glop for the tiles! You know something? That old fireplace is really amazing, you know what I mean? I can't believe that at first your mom had to drag me in there to help her! Now I feel like I'm right in the middle of some kind of mystery story, and I can hardly wait to see what we're going to find nex—"

"Spare me the details!" Deena broke in, cutting off the other girl mid-word. "I'll see that room when it's finished, and not two seconds sooner. I don't know why you're spending so much time in there anyway, when you could be singing with that boy Mike Iwasaki and those other people. He called you again this morning, but you're too rude to even call him back!"

As soon as she'd finished speaking, Deena was surprised at how crabby she'd sounded. What was wrong with her? She and Kathy had been getting along fairly well. Now she'd had to spoil it with a cutting remark about Mike Iwasaki—a subject she knew Kathy was touchy about for some reason. Deena didn't understand it, but the whole subject of the reading room project made her feel out of sorts and irritable.

She wondered if she should apologize for her nastiness. But when she turned toward Kathy, it was obvious that she already had her mind on other matters. Kathy was glued to the window, gazing open-mouthed at something on the front drive outside. Her hair dryer microphone and even Felix Freakout himself were completely forgotten.

"What on earth are you gaping at?" Deena asked. "Is Roy's crew working the front now?"

"I *wish*," Kathy breathed earnestly.

"You *wish* what exactly?" Deena asked. Honestly, sometimes Kathy's use of the English language was imprecise to the point of incomprehensibility!

"I *wish* Roy had a car like that! It is beyond awesome!"

"What kind of a car is that?" Deena asked absently. She wasn't really interested in cars, and as she'd been passing her desk, she'd glanced down at her letter to Whitney and realized she'd forgotten to sign it.

40

"I'm not sure, but I think it's a T-bird convertible. It's bright red, and I'll bet it's about twenty years old. But it looks brand-new."

"Really?" Deena wrote her name at the bottom of her letter and started toward the window. The description of the car was unusual enough to attract even a non-car buff's attention. "Can you see the driver?"

"No . . . yes! He's parking the T-bird and getting out. It's a guy. He's tall and thin, but he looks like he works out. He's got kind of swept-back brown hair with gray around the sides, but otherwise, he's really great looking. But you know what? The more I look at him, the more familiar he looks. I can't tell from way up here, but I think I may have seen him somewhere before. Hey! Maybe he's a movie star! But what would a movie star be doing here in the boonies with us? Come over here and check him out, Deena, and tell me who you think he is."

There was no response from her cousin, and Kathy wondered if she'd left the room. But when she turned around, she crashed right into Deena, who was standing a few inches behind her, staring fixedly out the window.

"Yikes!" Kathy cried. "You scared the socks off me! Why are you standing there like that anyway? Somebody glue you to the floor? What's the matter with you?"

Deena didn't say anything. She just kept on standing there, gazing out at the driveway. "What's the matter with you?" Kathy asked again. She was starting to feel alarmed. "Are you sick or something?"

Another silence followed. Then Deena seemed to pull herself together. "No . . . I'm not sick. But I don't feel well, if that's what you mean."

41

"Well, you don't *look* good, either. You should see your face. It's all kind of pale and white and weird. You look like you've just seen a ghost!"

Deena gave a quiet, unfunny little laugh. "In a way you're right," she said. "I have seen a ghost—if a ghost is something that vanishes into thin air when you least expect it."

Kathy was really starting to feel worried. She'd never heard her cousin sound like this. "Deena,"she said, "what in the world are you talking about?"

"That man out there. The one whose car you were drooling over. That man is my *father!*"

Chapter 5

The scenc at the bottom of the stairs looked like an old rerun of *Little House on the Prairie*. Lydia hadn't come back from the store yet, but everyone else was fussing around her ex-husband, Sam Scott, as if they were all part of a close-knit, loving family, and Sam was Pa, just returned from a lengthy trip through dangerous Indian country for supplies. Johnny, whom Sam had met only once, when Johnny was three years old, was pumping his uncle's hand and begging to be taken for ride in the Thunderbird. Kathy, who'd been hearing wild stories about Sam for most of her life, was gaping at the man as if he still might turn out to be the movie star she'd mistaken him for upstairs. And Nancy, who'd always enjoyed his company, was grinning at him and urging him to come in and sit down.

Only Deena hung back. After a quick hello and hurried hug from her father, she'd drifted away from the buzzing swarm in the doorway. Now she stood unnoticed in the shadows under the stairs. From her hiding place she observed her father with a mixture of adoration and resentment. She'd never felt so torn in her life. On the one hand she wanted to rush out again and throw herself back into Sam's arms. But on the other hand she wished she could quietly sink through the floorboards and disappear until her father was gone, safely out of her life. Just look at him, she said to herself. The perfect uncle, dropping in out of the blue and taking everybody by surprise. I wonder how long he'll stay around this time.

She continued standing there, unnoticed, while Sam laughed and chatted with the Manellis. As always, he immediately had everyone enchanted with the spell of his personality.

"This can't be little Johnny!" he exclaimed when he was reintroduced to his nephew. "I assumed this was a starter for the Boston Celtics! Come on and admit it, man! You're Larry Bird, staying here incognito to avoid your fans."

Johnny was struck dumb with pleasure. How could Uncle Sam have guessed how much he loved basketball? But now Sam was smiling at Kathy and reaching out to touch her safety pin necklace. "I might have known Nancy's daughter would turn out to be a real free spirit," he said. "Do you still sing as well as you did when you were a little girl?"

"Well, I hope so," Kathy said. "I mean, I sang with a band a few times this week. It went O.K., even though I'm not sure they're really the ones I should be singing with..."

"I'm sure we have a date...for you to sing and me to

44

listen!" her uncle interrupted. "That is, if there's a piano in this place?" He gazed around the lobby, taking in the polished wood floors and restored antique furniture. Then he turned to Nancy. "I have to hand it to you and Lydia," he told her earnestly. "You've really turned this place into a showplace. I wouldn't have believed it possible, but you've certainly done it!"

Nancy beamed as if she'd just won the Nobel Peace Prize. In her hiding place in the shadows Deena folded her arms in disgust. Typical, she said to herself. Within thirty seconds of his arrival, her father had managed to find the one thing each person was most proud of—and to purchase their lifelong devotion by praising it. Well, just let him try that ploy with her! He wouldn't find *her* so susceptible to his charms!

"But what are you doing here, Sam?" Nancy was saying. "I mean, hey, I know it's not your style to call in advance, but—"

"Oh, mellow out, Mom," Kathy broke in. "Uncle Sam just got here. Let him get in the door, at least, before you start giving him the third degree."

"No, no, Kathy," Sam said. "You're all definitely entitled to an explanation and an apology. The fact is, I couldn't let you know I was coming because I didn't know I was coming until yesterday. You see, I've signed on as a sales rep for a book company. The job starts next month, but I only just discovered this morning that Cranford was right outside the northern edge of my region! So I thought I might as well drive on up here and hang around until I have to hit the road and start selling my books. I've already booked a room over at the Inn of the Flying Goose and—"

"Sam?" Lydia's sharp voice came in from the front porch. "Sam?" She came into the entryway, clutching a small brown package and staring at her ex-husband in disbelief and annoyance. "What on earth are you doing here?"

Sam grinned and launched into a humorous, witty explanation about his new job. But after ten rocky years of marriage to the man, Lydia was immune to his charms. When he came to the part about staying in Cranford for a whole month, her mouth became a thin, set line.

"A whole month,"she repeated grimly. "Without any advance warning whatsoever. I must say, you haven't changed a bit Sam. You're still just as—"

"Lydia!" Nancy broke in hastily. "All that can wait . . . until later. When there aren't any *children* around!"

"Speaking of children," Johnny piped up, "I have a question. How come Uncle Sam has to stay at the Inn of the Flying Goose when we have about a million rooms right here in *this* inn?"

There was a short silence in the front hall. Then Nancy looked at her sister. "Johnny does have a point," she said. "We do have a lot of empty beds. What do you say, Lydia?"

Lydia folded her arms and sighed in exasperation. "I don't think it matters much what *I* say," she said. "Since I'm sure I'll be outvoted anyway. And I suppose it might be nice for Deena to have more than an occasional rare glimpse of her father while he's in the area." She turned toward her ex-husband. "Besides, the Flying Goose is outrageously expensive, Sam, and if you have that kind of money to throw around, I can think of a lot of other things you'd be well advised to invest in, such as Deena's college savings, or—"

"Speaking of Deena," Sam broke in, "where the heck did she go to, anyway?"

It's about time he noticed! Deena said to herself. "I've been right here the whole time, Daddy," she said, stepping out of the shadows.

"Well, then, come on over here and give your old dad another hug, Muffin," he said.

Deena took a few steps, determined to walk regally forward and greet her father with a polite but formal handshake. But when Sam held out both his arms, she immediately forgot all her resolutions and hurried into his embrace.

"I didn't have a chance to really look at you yet," Sam said after a minute. "Why, you're gorgeous! I'll bet you're knocking them dead at that new school you're going to. Any new heartthrobs these days?"

"Well, I thought so, but I'm not positive . . ."

"Come on, admit it, Muffin. Tell me how you've taken the place over."

"Well, if you *insist*, Daddy!" Deena responded with a shrill little laugh. "I haven't exactly taken over Cranford High, but I am in charge of the Spring Fling Entertainment Committee."

"That's my daughter! Now if only somebody would tell me what the Spring Fling Entertainment Committee is!"

Deena laughed again. "It's the committee that's responsible for selecting a theme for the Spring Fling. That's the dance the school holds each spring. I guess you'd have to say it's the biggest dance of the year." Even while Deena was speaking, she knew she sounded like a bragging idiot. But she was so rattled by her father's presence, she couldn't seem to make herself be quiet. Besides, Sam seemed to be eating it right up.

He squeezed Deena's shoulders. "I already know your theme ideas are real whoppers, Muffin. Let's hear all about them while you show your old dad to an empty room, O.K.?" He turned an inquiring glance toward his ex-wife. "That is, if you're positive it's O.K. for me to stay here, Lydia?"

Lydia shrugged and threw out her hands. "Take your father up to room three, Deena," she said. She looked at Sam. "It's vacant for now, so you might as well use it. But if we need the space for an unexpected guest, you'll have to go to the Flying Goose."

Sam thanked her and picked up his suitcase. Deena's bright, nervous chatter filled the front hall as she and her father started up the stairs. "Well, of course the dance is still in the planning stages, Daddy," Kathy heard her saying before the pair walked out of hearing range, "but I can tell you this. One person on the committee said she'd never heard ideas anything like mine before!"

At the bottom of the stairs Kathy snorted so loudly she almost choked. "You've got to be kidding!" she muttered. She couldn't believe her ears. Was Deena from another planet, or what? she asked herself. Could it possibly be for real that the other kids on that committee

48

had liked Deena's theme suggestions? It couldn't be true! Or if it was, then Cranford High was a lot nerdier than Kathy would have believed. Maybe it was time to start re-agitating for a transfer back to her old California high school. Mom hadn't bought that idea the first twelve times Kathy had suggested it, but a girl could always try again.

Anyway, there was no point in leaving till she found out if Deena had been telling Uncle Sam the truth. It had probably been a wild exaggeration—or maybe even an out and out lie! I mean, I'll believe it when I see it, Kathy thought. When I really *see* the gym looking like Bourbon Street, when I really *hear* authentic music from different periods in history . . . .

At that moment Kathy really did hear something. The old-fashioned phone on the table in the parlor was ringing. Kathy swung around, plunked herself down on the antique chair, propped her feet on top of the polished hall table, and picked up the phone. One of her dangling rhinestone earrings got in the way of the receiver, so she unhooked it and took it off before she said, "Hello?"

"Yo, Venus to Kathy! That you?"

"Yes, it's me," Kathy said. "Hi, Zee." She recognized Zee's voice with mixed feelings. Zee was usually pretty interesting, almost always getting herself into the middle of an intriguing situation, and Kathy loved intrigue.

But lately Kathy had been wondering exactly where Zee's head was at. Sometimes it seemed like Zee thought normal life was so boring, she had to go out and create her own intriguing situations if nothing particularly interesting happened to be going on in the world. This

49

made life exciting, of course, but it also made Kathy a little crazy. Life was weird enough, Kathy figured, without going out of your way to make it weirder.

"Anyway, Kath," the voice on the phone was going on after a loud *pop*! of chewing gum, "like I mean can you talk, or is the egghead standing right behind your shoulder or something?"

"The egghead?"

"Oh, get real"—chomp chomp—"You know who I mean. Your cousin, Ms. Perfect. God's gift to the teachers at Cranford High. Deena!"

"Right. Well, what do you want to know about her?"

"Well, I mean did she give you the poop on the dance committee, or what?"

"The dance committee?" Kathy repeated. "Deena didn't say anything about it to me."

"Oh." Zee sounded disappointed. "Well, I just thought she might be thinking about calling it off and running for principal instead, or something. I mean, the kids didn't exactly eat up her ideas with ketchup, if you know what I mean."

"She didn't say anything to me," Kathy said again.

"Well, let me know if she does, O.K.?" Zee said. "I mean I'll be absolutely hysterical if I'm not the first one in on the story, you dig?" She was making loud crying sounds into the phone as Kathy said good-by and hung up.

She put her earring back on, recrossed her feet on the table, and frowned. She was thinking about what she'd just said to Zee. It was the truth, she told herself. Deena hadn't said anything to *her* about the dance committee.

50

But Deena had said something to her father about it, and Kathy had heard every single bragging word. "I already know your theme ideas are real whoppers," Sam had said when Deena was gushing all over him about the committee meeting. He'd meant it in a nice way, of course. But he'd probably be pretty surprised, Kathy thought, if he knew that real whoppers were *exactly* what Deena had been telling him!

Chapter 6

For the thousandth time Deena silently cursed the Student Council for bribing this bunch of cretins to be on the entertainment committee. "All right, Trish!" she said through tightly clenched teeth. "Just stop saying you want a Bubble Gums tape again and again *ad nauseum*! You've made your wishes more than abundantly clear to all of us. Now please just be quiet for a minute, and *let me think!*"

Deena stopped talking and looked at Trish's injured wide-eyed stare. As a matter of fact, all the committee members, even Zack Rollins, were staring at her. Oh, no, she thought as she listened to the irritating loud hum of the overhead fluorescent lights. They think I've lost my mind. She cleared her throat and tried to think calmly. But it was difficult, especially with her angry words still bouncing off the dull gray walls of the multipurpose room.

She summoned up all her willpower. "Forgive me, Trish," she said with an apologetic smile. "I didn't mean to shout. It's just that I've been under a certain amount of stress lately . . ." Her voice trailed off, and she became lost in thought. As she propped her elbows on the table and rested her weary chin on her hands, she considered what she'd just said. It was definitely the understatement of the millennium. Since her father had arrived five days ago, she'd felt as if she were living in a constant state of confusion and mental strain. And the thing that made it even more frustrating was that she couldn't figure out *why* she felt that way! It certainly wasn't true for anyone else in the house. Even her mother seemed to be enjoying his visit and was more relaxed than she'd been since the divorce. And the rest of them had been having the times of their lives, listening with open mouths to Sam's endless supply of stories about his various careers, travels, and adventures, giggling hysterically at his imitations of the strange characters he'd met along the way, laughing at the impulsive, lighthearted things he did, like ordering out for a pizza supreme with anchovies at two a.m. or performing *The Wizard of Oz* all by himself in the front parlor, using a different voice for each character. It should have been great having Dad around for a whole month—wild, wacky, and wonderful. And it was. But also it wasn't. And Deena just couldn't understand why. If only she could figure it all out . . .

"Oh, Deena darling!" The cooing voice snapped Deena out of her reverie so suddenly, her elbows slipped, and she caught herself just before she cracked her chin on the tabletop. Her sudden movement caused her pile of folders to crash onto the floor at her feet.

"Pardon us, Deena, dear," Zee repeated in a voice dripping with fake concern. "If you'd like to be by yourself, that's perfectly cool with us! The rest of us can go on off and have the meeting without you."

"Uh...no...that won't be necessary," Deena said from under the table, where she was scrambling around, frantically picking up folders. "Everything's under complete control. But...that is to say...could someone please remind me of what we were just talking about?"

"Putting together some Bubble Gums tapes," Trish Boswell repeated patiently. "And a good punch recipe."

Flustered, Deena resumed her seat and cleared her throat once again. "Ah, yes," she said. "Bubbie Gums tapes." She gazed around the table again, desperately trying to figure out what to do. She knew she was in big trouble. Besides Zee, who didn't bear thinking about, the only person on the committee with an idea in her so-called mind was Trish. Zack was drifting off to sleep again, Steve was punching figures into his laptop computer, and Rainier's eyes were looking even more glazed over than usual. And to make matters worse, Sally Brown seemed to be getting ready to leave. "Track practice," she said abruptly, unfolding her long, strong legs and getting to her feet. "Got to leave. Let me know what you decide."

"But Sally," Deena called to the other girl's departing back, "you haven't told us what sort of theme you want for the dance."

"Oh, don't much care," Sally said as she opened the door. "Can't come to the dance myself. Got hockey camp that weekend."

Oh, that's just marvelous, Deena thought bitterly. One of the committee members wasn't even coming to the dance. All anyone else could suggest was a tape recorder on the stage, some punch, and some malodorous paper flowers. And that uninspired idea was undoubtedly what the other committee members would vote for, since it would involve the least amount of effort on their parts. And unless she gave in to the will of the majority, she'd have a mutiny on her hands. The only problem was, if she went along with their wishes, she'd feel as if she'd lowered her own standards. She wouldn't even want to go to the dance!

She decided to try one more thing. In desperation she turned toward Trish Boswell, the only committee member besides Zee who seemed to be paying attention to what was going on. "Listen, Trish," she said, "I admit my ideas may have been too ... too ambitious. Too much work for everybody. But ... a bunch of taped music on the stage ... don't you think we could at least try to find a real band? We could ... "

She stopped talking when she became aware of a newcomer standing in the doorway of the multipurpose room. She looked up and felt her pulse quicken when she saw that it was Ken Buckly, just back from his week at the state capital.

As usual, she couldn't see Ken without being struck by how incredibly good-looking he was, with his tall, strong body, blond hair, and blue eyes. After a week away from Cranford he looked better than ever.

When Ken saw her looking at him, he gave her a little half-smile that made her flush with pleasure. But her first rush of happiness was cut off when she suddenly wondered just how long Ken had been standing there, listening in the doorway. Had he noticed what was going on in the meeting? Had he seen how bored the people on the committee were? Had he observed how Deena was compulsively knotting and unknotting a lock of her hair till it looked like the tail end of a witch's broom?

Suddenly she was overcome with the need to do something to make herself look good, to make it appear that she had some kind of control over the meeting. Before she really knew what was happening, Deena heard herself saying, "Look, if all you people want is some plain rock music and some punch, then so be it. But I think we should have a live band, and I'm going to find one! By this time next week I will have checked out some bands, and I will submit their names to you for your approval." To her amazement her voice was firm, decisive, and sure of itself. But her heart and stomach knew better. Inside her body her vital organs were slowly sinking to the soles of her feet.

"Miss Classical Music U.S.A. is going to find a rock band?" Zee's voice sounded disbelieving—and also disappointed at Deena's sudden burst of authority, as if she'd been looking forward to seeing Deena collapse on the floor, begging for a straitjacket and a padded wagon from the state hospital.

"Yes, I am!" Deena closed her top folder with an efficient snap.

"Get real," Zee said, clearly indicating that she didn't believe this one was possible. "But I guess that means we'd better meet again early next week. I mean, if we're *really* getting to choose from a whole fistful of bands, we'll need to pick which one we want, plus decide on decorations and stuff. After all, the dance is less than three weeks away." She leaned forward into the light, and the bright green streak in her hair glowed as if it were radioactive plutonium. "Does that give you enough time, darling chairperson?" she asked innocently. "If we meet again . . . say Monday afternoon?"

"Yes, of course," Deena answered, but more slowly this time. Good grief, she thought, Zee was some kind of monster in a human body! "We'll meet again in three days."

The committee members started to their feet, and Deena looked over in Ken's direction to see what kind of impression she'd made on him with her authority and voice of assurance. But to her surprise and disappointment, the doorway was empty! Ken was gone!

Deena felt sick. Had she gone through the entire charade of pretending she knew how to find a rock band for nothing? Hastily she grabbed up all her folders and hurried toward the door. When she came out into the hall she caught sight of Ken disappearing around the corner.

"Ken!" she called. As soon as she'd shouted his name, she felt her cheeks begin to burn. What is Ken going to think of you? she asked herself. Shrieking after him like a screeching cat! He'll probably pretend not to hear and keep right on going.

But Ken didn't keep right on going. He was turning around and heading in Deena's direction. "Hi, there," he called. "I was going to wait for your meeting to break up, but it looked like it might go on all night, so I thought I'd catch you later instead. I'm so hassled right now, I feel like I can't waste a minute."

"Well, we finished quickly," Deena said, going to meet him. As always, she felt her heart begin to thump as she looked up at Ken's clear blue eyes. "What's got you so hassled?"

Ken held out the pile of books and papers under his arm. "Homework mainly," he said. "I have to make up all the stuff I missed when I was out of town."

"Oh, dear. So how was the govern—"

"Yoo-hoo, Ken!" A stunning red-haired senior girl named Wendy Blair rudely interrupted the conversation without a single *Excuse me*. Deena clamped her mouth shut with a snap.

"Mr. Anderson sent me to see if you were still in the building, Ken," Wendy gushed. "The printer in the computer lab is jammed up again, and he says you're the only one who can get it working again."

Ken glanced at his watch and sighed. "Well, I guess I can spare a minute if it's a real crisis."

"Oh, it *is*, Ken! That's the very word Mr. Anderson used!" Wendy flashed a gorgeous, pearly white smile as she took Ken's arm, mashed herself up against his side, and started hauling him away. "You're our hero!"

Ken twisted his head around and gave Deena an apologetic, backward look over his shoulder. She smiled, shrugged, and gave him a perky wave as if she didn't have a care in the world. But in her heart she felt alone and forlorn.

She watched Ken's and Wendy's departing figures until they were out of sight. She had to admit Wendy was attractive with that bright shiny hair and that short, tight skirt. Deena looked down at her own wool slacks and sweater and wondered if she should change her image. Maybe she would get a little more attention around here if she looked more like Wendy Blair—or even Kathy Manelli, for that matter.

A sudden idea came to her, and she hurried toward her locker to get the rest of her books. Once outside the school she started in the direction of the drugstore. She stopped short when she saw Ace Lardner and his pals hanging around in the parking lot, heckling people as usual. She ducked back inside the school building and left through another exit.

You'd think the faculty would do something about Ace and those thugs, she thought again as she wound in and out through the quaint little Cranford streets. Or the town council or *somebody*.

She turned down Main Street and went into White's Pharmacy, where she began searching for the hair care aisle. When she found it, she spent several long minutes studying the different types of hair-color mousse. "Aha!" she said at last. "Shimmering Saffron, for golden, sunlit highlights in blond hair."

She picked up two boxes and carried them to the counter, along with a selection of iridescent eyeshadow and vivid nailpolish. "I'm not sure if I'll actually use any of these products," she explained to the woman behind the register. "But it never hurts to be prepared for an image change!"

The woman yawned and rang up the purchase as if she hadn't heard a word Deena had said. As she went back out onto Main Street, Deena felt a new wave of depression wash over her. She must have become invisible or something. Even the cashier in the drugstore was ignoring her now!

Stuffing her bag of cosmetics into her oversized leather shoulder bag, she trudged back the way she'd come, circling the school and turning onto the street that led toward home. As she walked, she went over her list of woes again and again. By the time she could see the inn, she felt so sorry for herself, she was almost in tears.

All at once she couldn't take it anymore. Everything was going wrong. She felt just the way she had when she was seven years old and had fallen off her bike and scraped her knees. She wanted her mother. She'd gotten herself into a stupid situation, but it was nothing that couldn't be worked out. Mom was the most level-headed person in the universe. She'd know exactly what to do to straighten out this mess.

With that thought in mind Deena hurried inside, threw her books and shoulder bag on the hall table, and went to the kitchen in search of her mother. Once again she found only Johnny, happily stirring something in a bowl.

She didn't stop to examine whatever nauseating concoction he was mixing this time. Instead, she turned around, went back through the dining room and hurried upstairs.

"Mom!" she called. No answer. She tapped on the door of her mother's bedroom, but got no response. She was starting downstairs again when she heard it. *Scritchety, scratchety, scritch*. It was coming from the vacant guest room, the soon-to-be upstairs reading room.

Deena couldn't believe her ears. Mom and Kathy were *still* secluded in there, happily scraping plaster together? Why, Kathy had spent more time with Deena's mother in the past week than she had with her own mother in the past *year*! Kathy and Mom had become a veritable fireplace restoration *team*! But how long could their never-ending project last? If Kathy spent a fraction of that amount of time doing her homework, she'd be class valedictorian!

Deena shook her head and stood irresolutely in the upstairs hall. She knew that if she burst into the guest room and told her mother she was upset, her mother would come out and listen to her problems. But talking to an irritable, distracted, plaster-covered Mom wasn't exactly what Deena had in mind. She wanted her mother's undivided, concentrated, thoughtful attention.

No, she told herself. Mom would have to wait. She'd go downstairs, collect her homework, and concentrate on that until Mom and *dear cousin* Kathy were finished for the day.

As she started back down the stairs, the acrid smell of scorched dill pickles and sauerkraut drifted toward her from the kitchen. Johnny! If someone didn't stop that poor kid from using the stove, he was surely going to hurt himself!

She picked up her speed, intending to charge into the kitchen and give her little cousin a kind but stern lecture about stove safety. But as she reached the bottom of the staircase, she stopped. What was that sound coming from the front parlor? Was it music?

"Doo-wah-de-dippity-dip," a voice sang. A few more off-key notes thumped out. That piano needed a good tuning. "Singing doo-doo-de-waaaaah . . . "

Was that Daddy's voice? Deena wondered.

"Dum, diddee, doo . . . "

It was her father's voice! She should have recognized it at once. Sam Scott had always had a rich, distinctive singing voice. In fact, right after he'd graduated from college, he'd actually performed as a keyboard player and back-up singer with a group of other musicians called the Teen Dreamers or something. It had been before Deena was born, but she'd heard all about it. Some of Sam's funniest stories were about that period of his life.

An idea sprang fully-formed into Deena's head. Daddy! Her father knew all about music and rock bands and things of that nature. Of course he didn't perform himself anymore, but he always kept current with anything he'd once been involved in. He was the perfect person to advise her about how to locate a band.

She had just started toward the front parlor when a sudden thought stopped her. Why had she boasted to her father at such length about her authority and influence with the entertainment committee? If she came to him now, begging for help, wouldn't he realize it had all been one enormous lie after another?

Oh, so what if he did! she told herself sharply. If she kept worrying about that, she'd never get herself out of this corner she'd painted herself into. Besides, the man was her father and was obligated to love her no matter how stupidly she acted!

With renewed determination, she turned toward the parlor and threw open the door. She marched inside and opened her mouth to speak. Then she stopped short. Oh, no! This had to be seen to be believed. It was too much to bear!

"She loves him, bop-she-wop!" Sam Scott was indeed singing old songs and thumping out an accompaniment on the out-of-tune piano. But he wasn't doing it by himself. Snuggled up close to him, singing and playing her heart out, was Kathy. From the look on Kathy's face, she'd never been happier in her life.

Without saying a word or making a sound, Deena whirled around and fled from the parlor. She ran back up the stairs, yanked open the door to her room, and threw herself face down on her bed. As she sobbed into her pillow, she could still hear the strains of music drifting upward from the parlor below.

Chapter 7

About an hour later Kathy wandered into the bedroom, sat on her bed, pulled off her high top wrestling shoes, and flung each one into a different corner. By this time Deena was sitting up at her desk, hunched over her homework in a pose of intense concentration. But from her red eyes, blotchy face, and shuddering breathing, Kathy could tell her cousin had been crying about something.

Maybe Ken asked somebody else to the Spring Fling, Kathy thought. Or else Deena was bummed out about that Spring Fling dance committee. Kathy had run into Zee in the hall that day, and her friend had gleefully told her she thought Deena was headed for Disaster City, U.S.A. "Can you dig it? Little Miss Out-of-It says *she's* going to find a band!" Zee had chortled. "But I think she's pulling a bluff. And I also think anyone who wants music at the Spring Fling had better come toting their own kazoos!"

Kathy couldn't keep from laughing at the image of the whole school grooving to kazoo music, but in her heart she'd felt worried sick. *Deena* was promising to find a rock band? Deena could hardly tell the difference between a rock band and a *rubber* band! Kathy thought of offering to ask Dementia to play at the dance. But she rejected the idea as soon as she thought of it. For one thing Dementia's music was too punked-out for most of the dance crowd. But also Kathy still hadn't worked out her *own* feelings about singing with that band. True, their jam sessions this week had been pretty hot. But it hadn't been the same as playing with the kids back home. Kathy still didn't feel ready for a public performance.

Just then Deena inhaled a long, quavering breath and shuddered inside her pale green turtleneck and color-coordinated cardigan. Kathy was surprised to feel a pang of sympathy for her cousin. Even though the Spring Fling fiasco was all Deena's fault, the situation was still a real downer. Her cousin had totally painted herself into a corner and now she was stuck there. Kathy was annoyed with her, but she could still feel sorry for her. With a sudden burst of good will she decided to try to cheer Deena up.

"You know something, Deena?" she asked. As she spoke, she kicked a pile of clutter off her bed so she could lie down and stretch out her long legs. She gazed with satisfaction at her skin-tight, torn-at-the-knee, acid-washed jeans and oversized bleached sweat shirt. "You're really lucky."

"And why is that, may I ask?"

"Because you've got such a great dad, of course!"

"Oh."

"I mean, my dad was great, too, and I really miss him and all," Kathy went on. "But he wasn't anything like your dad. Uncle Sam is cool. And he can do absolutely everything!"

"He's certainly tried to do everything," Deena said dryly. "Mom says that's because he gets bored fast, and he can't see any *one* thing through to the finish."

"Well, it sure makes him interesting," Kathy chattered on. "And he's so funny, too, and he drives such a terrific car. And he has such great clothes. I mean, it's like he's in our—I mean *my* generation. He doesn't even seem like a real dad."

"I know what you mean about that," Deena said in a quiet voice.

"He's had such unbelievable experiences! Did you know he once played keyboard for a real band? He's really a great musician. We were playing together downstairs just now, and—"

Deena swallowed hard and interrupted with a quick rush of words. "Kathy, speaking of music, there's something I need to ask you ... "

Kathy didn't notice the desperate tone of Deena's voice. Instead she glanced at her three gigantic plastic watches and sat up. "I'd love to talk to you, Deena, I really would. But would you mind waiting till after we eat tonight? I promised your mom I'd help her chip off the last section of plaster on the fireplace this afternoon, but then I got busy singing and I forgot. If I run in there now, I can see what she's uncovered."

66

Without waiting for an answer, she bounced off her bed and hurried out of the room. If she'd waited two seconds longer, she would have seen her cousin put her head down on her desk and bury her face in her arms.

Chapter 8

The silverware gleamed, the china plates glittered, and the happy, chattering faces glowed in the soft candlelight. Outside in the dining room the guests could be heard gently clinking their forks against their plates as they talked and ate. Around the scarred wooden kitchen table the conversation was lively and enthusiastic. Sam had made dinner that night, so instead of one of Nancy's crunchy, grainy health food meals, the family was eating rich, creamy pasta carbonara with buttery garlic bread and Caesar salad. Everything was delicious. It was a scene that could have been photographed for the glossy pages of *Gourmet* magazine.

No one noticed that two people in the scene weren't eating, talking, or glowing. At one end of the table Johnny sat slouched down in his chair, using his bread to smush all his pasta together into a mushy, sloppy heap in the middle of his plate. The corners of his mouth were turned down, his eyes were drooping, and his face was pale and slightly greenish. If the room had been a little quieter, someone might have heard some ominous grumbling sounds coming from the direction of his stomach.

At the other end of the table Deena also looked unhappy. She had taken one bite of salad and then quietly folded her hands in her lap. Every now and then she drank a few sips of water from her glass, but she didn't try to eat anything else. As she sat quietly in her chair, the expression in her eyes was slowly changing from anxiety to anger as she listened to the others' conversation.

"Five more days!" Lydia was saying enthusiastically. "In five more days the reading room will be ready. Two days to finish polishing up the fireplace, and three to put up shelves and haul cast-off furniture down from the attic. Don't you think that's about right, Kathy?"

"Yeah, I guess so. Though we're going to need some help lugging down all that stuff. That old attic stairway looks like something right out of *Friday the Thirteenth, part twelve*!"

"Well, I never would have believed it," Nancy put in as she served herself a second helping of pasta. "Kathy, I'm really pleased with the way you've helped Lydia with that room. It was hard work, but you really stuck with it—though, from all the laughing and talking I heard through the door, it sounded as if the two of you were having a party in there!"

"It wasn't exactly my idea of a *party*," said Kathy with a mouthful of bread. "But it was fun. Though not as much fun as singing those songs with you this afternoon, Uncle Sam!"

"That was terrific, wasn't it?" Sam agreed. "Though I think we need to spend a little more time on the harmony on the chorus of 'Teen Angel.' We were so off-key, we sounded like a pair of constipated coyotes!"

Kathy laughed so hard, she sprayed herself and Deena with a million tiny pieces of chewed-up bread. Deena gasped in outrage and then slowly and deliberately wiped herself off with her napkin. She glared at her cousin, who was still choking with laughter. "Sorry," Kathy said, reaching for her water glass. "But those constipated coyotes cracked me right up. I guess we did sound pretty bad. Maybe we could practice some more after dinner. O.K., Uncle Sam?"

"Sure, Kathy."

"As soon as you help with the dishes, that is," Lydia reminded them.

Just then Nancy noticed the mountain of food on Johnny's plate. "Speaking of constipated," she said, "are you all right, Johnny? You haven't eaten a bite, and your face is sort of a strange color."

"Hey!" Kathy said. "I have some eyeshadow like that. It's called Shocking Chartreuse. The kid's face is exactly the same shade!"

"Shut up, Kathy," Johnny said in a strangled voice. "I'm just not hungry, that's all. I made myself a snack after school, and now I think I'm gonna be . . . " Before he could finish his announcement, he threw himself backward out of his chair and bolted out of the room.

Nancy glanced around the table, put out her hands, and shrugged. Then she got to her feet and hurried after her son.

There was a moment's silence. "Well, for heaven's sake," Lydia said. "I wonder what he could have eaten to make himself so sick."

"Sauerkraut and pickles!" Deena said in a loud, indignant voice. "And undoubtedly whatever else he could lay his hands on in the kitchen. It's disgusting, that's what it is. That child is left without any sort of supervision whatsoever in the afternoons—he must rely on his own devices to feed himself, to entertain himself, to clothe and house himself . . ."

"To clothe and house himself?" Lydia said in surprise. "Aren't you getting a little carried away, Deena?"

"Well, you know what I mean. No one ever pays any attention to that child anymore. And I for one am not the slightest bit surprised he's finally poisoned himself. I'm only relieved he hasn't burned the inn down around our ears!"

There was another much longer, much more uncomfortable silence. Then Sam glanced over at the uneaten food on Deena's plate. "It looks like Johnny's not the only one who's not hungry tonight. Did he share his sauerkraut and pickles with you this afternoon, Muffin?"

Lydia and Kathy started to smile at the image of the fastidious Deena eating anything so gross, but they stopped when Deena banged her fist on the table and barked out a short, abrupt, "No!"

Sam cleared his throat and tried again. "You've been

so busy doing your homework, you haven't been keeping me up to date on your life, Muffin," he said, reaching out to pat Deena's hand.

"I'm not the only one who's been busy lately," Deena said, glowering around the table. Her voice was low and ominous.

Sam pretended not to notice his daughter's hostile tones. "I've been wondering," he said pleasantly. "How are things going with your love life? And with that big committee you're the head honcho of?"

To everyone's astonishment Deena snatched her hand away from her father's, jumped to her feet, and flung her napkin onto her food. As she leaped up, she banged into the table. The pitcher of ice water next to her plate teetered and then crashed over on top of the salad bowl. A revolting combination of ice water and Italian dressing flooded across the wooden tabletop, but no one made a move to clean it up. Everyone sat motionless, staring in shock at Deena.

"I don't have a love life!" she shouted. "And the committee's going rotten! Downhill, down the tubes, right into the bottom of the rat-infested sewer where it belongs!"

"Deena honey . . . "

Deena ignored her mother's soothing voice. "But so what?" she cried. "What do I care what happens to a stupid old committee? Why should I care about anything I do? Nobody *else* around here does!"

With that Deena burst into tears and stumbled blindly out of the room, knocking over her chair as she went. For a minute Lydia, Sam, and Kathy stayed sitting at the table, gaping at each other in astonishment. Then Lydia pushed back her chair and started to her feet. "Oh, dear," she said. "I wonder what on earth could have happened to upset her this much? I'm going after her."

Kathy put a hand on her aunt's arm. "I'd better go instead," she said as she stood up. "I think I might know what's going on with her."

She left the kitchen and followed her cousin up to their room on the third floor. She found Deena crying and pacing back and forth on their hardwood floor. "What's the matter?" Kathy asked.

Deena stopped pacing and glared at Kathy. "How can ... you ... stand there ... " Deena said in the intervals between her long, heaving sobs, "and ... ask me that? You know what's the matter. And ... it's all ... your fault!"

Kathy's mouth fell open. "*My* fault? What did *I* do?"

"You ... you ... you," Deena gulped in air in an effort to control her crying. "First your friend Zee ... then Mom ... then Da ... d ... dy ... then K ... K ... Ken ... oh, go away! I can't talk now."

Without saying anything Kathy marched into the tiny bathroom off their room. A few seconds later she returned with a glass of water. "Drink this," she ordered. "And stop choking like that. We haven't gotten to the Heimlich maneuver in health class yet."

"The Heimlich maneuver is for choking on *food*," Deena said as she reached for the water.

"Well, now I feel better. If you can remember to correct my mistakes, you can't have totally flipped your

73

lid. There must still be a few working brain cells in there."

In spite of her anger Deena smiled through her tears at the joke. She drank a half glass of water and sat down on her bed.

"That's better," Kathy said. "Now tell me why it's my fault that you suddenly went insane downstairs and tried to drown the dinner table."

"I guess everything just came together at once," Deena said. "And I exploded."

"But what's the *matter*?" Kathy asked again.

"You won't understand."

"Well, I admit I don't usually understand what you're talking about. But if you're willing to try to explain in normal English, I'm willing to try to listen."

"Oh, all right. But it's hard for me to explain, because I'm not sure I really understand it myself. Mainly, I think it has to do with my father. It's very upsetting for me to have him here."

Kathy planted her hands on her hips and shook her head. "I was wrong before," she said. "You have totally flipped your lid. Your father is great!"

"You see?" Deena started crying again. "I told you you wouldn't understand!"

"All right, all right, all right!" Kathy said hastily. "I'm sorry. I just can't understand why having Uncle Sam here would be upsetting for you. You admit he's funny, and nice, and sweet, and a definite ten on the looks scale, don't you?"

"Oh, yes," Deena said. "He's all those things and more. That's part of the problem."

Kathy sighed and sat down on her desk chair. She jumped up again when she realized she'd sat on her wire hairbrush. She threw it on the floor and sat down for a second time. "I think you'd better start from the beginning," she said.

Deena reached for a tissue and blew her nose. "All right," she said. "You see, it's precisely as you were just saying. My father has always been the funniest, sweetest, most handsome father around."

"But?"

"But the problem is that he almost never *is* around! At least not very often."

"But he's staying here for a whole month."

"Right!" Deena responded. "He's here for a month, and everyone's fallen in love with him. But where has he been for the last *eight* months since we've been here? And why hasn't he called me or written me during that whole time?"

"Oh!" Kathy stared across the room at her cousin. "Oh. So you mean . . . "

"All at once, from time to time, without any warning whatsoever, he waltzes into my life and wants to be part of our family again. And of course I love him and I'm happy to see him . . . but, but . . . "

"But you know if you let yourself get all hung up on him again, he'll just . . . "

"Disappear again," Deena finished sadly. "He always has, and he always will. That's why I get so mixed up and talk so crazily whenever he asks me about school or boys or anything. I feel that if he honestly wanted to know about my real life, he'd stay in closer touch with me all the time. But also I seem to have some irrational need to attract his attention—to be the image of the perfect daughter for him. You may not believe this, Kathy, but upon occasion I've actually found myself telling Daddy things that aren't . . . well, entirely accurate—so he'll be impressed with me."

Kathy remembered what she'd heard Deena telling Uncle Sam about the Spring Fling Entertainment Committee. "I believe you, Deena," she said.

Her cousin shook her head. "It's all so terribly confusing," she said with a sigh.

Kathy was quiet for a minute, frowning as she concentrated on her own thoughts. Then her face brightened. "Maybe you could talk to him about it!" she said excitedly. "Maybe he just doesn't understand how you feel. Maybe he could change."

A weary smile came onto Deena's tear-streaked face. "He won't change, Kathy. He simply does not realize the effect his behavior has on other people."

"I still think you should try talking to him. What harm can it do?"

"My mother tried talking to him for ten years of marriage, but she finally learned her lesson. Even she still admits that Daddy is a warm, wonderful person. But he's also *restless*. And unreliable."

Kathy got to her feet and came over to sit next to her cousin on the bed. "That's rough, Deena," she said. "I guess that sort of explains why Aunt Lydia sometimes seems a little . . ."

"I believe the expression you'd use is *uptight*. She tried for ten years to get my father to be responsible and reliable, but she was finally defeated. I think she may be afraid I'll turn out like him, or something, so she watches me like a hawk to be sure I always do the right thing."

"But you always *do* do the right thing! It drives me crazy!"

"I know I do. I can't stop myself. Whenever I think of breaking even the tiniest of rules—say, of going to bed without brushing my teeth or staying out past curfew like you do all the time—I think of how disappointed Mom would be, and I kill myself trying to be letter-perfect. I just can't help being a hopeless Goody Two-shoes!"

Since Goody Two-shoes was one of Kathy's favorite private nicknames for Deena, she couldn't help chuckling out loud even though she felt sympathetic. "Oh, well," she said. "There are worse things to be than too good . . . I *guess*. Besides, even though your dad isn't always here for you, your mom sure is. She may not be perfect, but she's always around."

"She used to be always around," Deena said. "But not lately. I've been trying to talk to her all week, but she's been so obsessed with remodeling that reading room with you, she's barely even noticed!"

"Oh. Oh. I guess maybe I should have noticed you were trying to get through to her in there." Kathy paused and cleared her throat. "Were you trying to tell your mom about the flack you're getting from the Spring Fling committee kids?"

"You knew about that!" Deena burst out in surprise. "Zee must have told you."

"Yeah, she did," Kathy admitted. "Though even before that, when you told me those ideas of yours, I was

77

afraid the kids might think they were kind of weird. A bit too far-out, you might say."

"Far-out is the understatement of the year!" Deena admitted ruefully. "It would have taken a Hollywood production crew a year to set up one of those ideas." She got up and wandered into the bathroom to splash cold water on her red, swollen eyes. "But still," she said, coming out with a wet washcloth in her hand, "my most absurd idea is a hundred times better than what the committee's come up with. Trish Boswell is the only one in the whole group who'll even speak at the meetings. And all she wants is the same old thing—a tape player and some punch, a tape player and some punch. I know I could save myself a lot of mental grief by just giving in and doing what she wants. But how can I face myself in the mirror, knowing that a committee chaired by Deena Scott could conceive of nothing more inspired than that?"

Kathy made a face at Deena's lofty language. The girl sounded like she was planning the next royal wedding! She was about to make her usual snotty remark when she remembered all the stuff Deena had just told her about her mother and father. For a lot of upsetting, far-out reasons, the Spring Fling committee had become really important to her cousin. Kathy would be a total jerk if she didn't help her now. Besides, Deena did have a point.

Thoughtfully Kathy nodded her spiky head. "It'd be a real drag to settle for the same old junk they've always had," she agreed. "What we have to do is this: come up with a theme that's interesting and a little different . . . "

"Exactly what I've been saying!" Deena interrupted.

She opened her mouth to go on, but Kathy continued with her speech.

"*But* it also has to be something that the kids can really get into. With a good band and a really far-out theme—that's not too far-out. That means nothing too brainy or intellectual. No historical productions or Mardi Gras."

"I completely agree with you. We need a theme that has a popular, slightly lowbrow appeal. And we need to find a real-live breathing band."

Now it was Kathy's turn to start pacing back and forth across the wood floor. As she walked, she hummed little pieces of songs to herself and absent-mindedly kicked her clothes and shoes out of her path. Deena was sitting on the bed again, clutching her washcloth and frowning in intense concentration. The room was absolutely quiet, except for the sound of Kathy's humming and the sound of her high-tops, squeaking as she moved to and fro across the wooden floorboards.

Then, without Kathy's realizing it, an idea began to grow in her mind. Her quiet humming began growing louder. As she paced, she started singing the words to one of the songs she and Sam had been practicing that afternoon. "Rock, rock, rock, baby, rock and roll with me."

She stopped singing, but the lyrics seemed to hang in the air like a dangling lightbulb. Then *squeak*! Kathy's sneakers skidded to a stop. She made up her mind. "Deena!" she announced. "I have the answer!"

Chapter 9

Twenty minutes and one excited, borderline hysterical conversation later, Deena and Kathy raced down the stairs and flew into the kitchen in search of Sam. They found their prey, washing dishes, drinking coffee, and talking earnestly with Lydia and Nancy. The expressions on all three adults' faces were serious and worried.

As soon as Sam saw Deena, he put down his coffee mug and turned away from the soap sink. "Muffin," he said. "Deena. I want to ask you ... that is, I'm not sure I understand what I said to make you ... ?"

"I appreciate what you're trying to say, Daddy," she said. "And I do want to have a long talk sometime soon. But right now Kathy has something urgent she needs to discuss with you."

Sam listened to Deena's breathless, happy voice and looked at her flushed, animated face, and his eyes grew wide. Nancy and Lydia both clutched their steaming coffee mugs and stared at each other in complete bewilderment. What had happened to the irrational, sobbing girl who'd flown into a fit of rage and rushed out of the room less than an hour ago?

"But, Muffin," Sam said. "I want to find out how I—"

"Later, Daddy!" Deena said. "But right now you have to listen to Kathy's idea." She grabbed one of his hands and started pulling him out of the kitchen and through the dining room, right past the eyes of a middle-aged couple from Manhattan who were lingering over their pineapple upside-down cake. As Sam went by, he shot a desperate, quizzical, backward glance over his shoulder at Lydia and Nancy. But they didn't know any more than he did. All they could do was shake their heads and send up silent prayers that their daughters hadn't suddenly, simultaneously gone insane.

Deena hauled Sam into the front parlor and sat him down on the piano bench. "It's like this, Uncle Sam," Kathy began as she sprawled out on one of the Victorian loveseats. "It's a new idea for the Spring Fling—you remember, the dance we're having at school?"

Sam looked more bewildered than ever. "*That's* what this urgent conversation is about? But I thought that was all settled. I understood the committee was going ahead with one of the ideas Deena already presented."

Deena blushed, stared at the rag rug, and started to stammer an explanation but before she got out two words, Kathy tried to save her from having to make an embarrassing confession. "Everyone thought those ideas were terrific, of course," she said with an elaborate yawn. "They'd never heard anything like them. But . . . but . . . " she went on, thinking quickly, "so . . . so . . . "

"So!" Deena broke in. "So what really happened is that they all hated my ideas, and I stupidly promised to find a rock band without having the smallest clue of how to go about it. But Kathy just reminded me that she's actually *in* a rock band right now!"

"Well," Kathy put in doubtfully, thinking of her informal sessions with Mike Iwasaki and Dementia, "I wouldn't exactly say I'm in a band . . . or that it's even really a band at all yet, or . . . "

Deena brushed away her objections. "But with some work you could be a band, right, Kathy? Isn't that what you said upstairs?"

Kathy nodded. "That's what I said," she admitted, beginning to wonder what had possessed her upstairs. "It would take a lot of work, but I think Mike and I would be able to pull the group together if we really concentrated on it."

"That's terrific, Kathy!" said Sam. "It sounds like you've really helped Muffin here out of a sticky situation. But where do I fit into all of this? Why did you two kidnap me and drag me in here?"

"Because we've got a major problem, Uncle Sam!" Kathy explained. "Mike Iwasaki and those other guys only play really heavy-duty metal music. It's fantastic—but just too radical for the mainstream. It would never go over at an all-school function like the Spring Fling."

"It would be unbearable!" Deena agreed. "Simply odious."

Kathy shot her cousin a look. "So my idea is to get Dementia to change their style a bit for the dance. I want to convince them to play songs from the fifties and sixties …"

"So we can have a Golden Oldies Spring Fling!" Deena concluded enthusiastically. "What do you think, Daddy?"

Sam rubbed his lean, handsome face with his hand. "It sounds like a fine idea to me," he said. "Nostalgia is really *in* these days, I believe. But you still haven't answered my question, girls. Where do I fit into all this?"

Kathy got to her feet and faced her uncle. "Don't you see, Uncle Sam? We can't do it without you. None of those kids in Dementia know any of those old songs. But you do! You used to actually perform them! You'd be the perfect one to teach us."

Sam's expression changed from one of confusion to one of anxiety. "Teach you?" he said. "Oh, I don't know about that. You say the dance is only a few weeks away? I'm not sure there's enough time. And besides, I'm not much of a teacher."

"You're a great teacher!" Kathy cried. "You taught me a whole lot in just a couple of hours this afternoon! You told me you'd never forget all those great old songs."

Sam looked thoughtful for a long minute. "I suppose it's just possible we could pull it off," he said slowly. "I wish I had my old music trunk with me, but it's in a storage bin in Manhattan. It's got all my music from the old days. I think I still have my Teen Dreamers uniforms packed up down there, if the moths haven't gotten to them."

"Your group was called the Teen Dreamers?" Kathy asked in disbelief.

Sam laughed. "It certainly was. The name was printed right on the backs of our shiny pink shirts. We thought we were cool cats back then."

Kathy moved a step closer to her uncle. "Does this trip down memory lane mean you'll help us with the dance, Uncle Sam?" she asked. "If I can convince Dementia to go along with my idea?"

"I admit it sounds like fun," Sam said. "But it's a pretty big commitment. And I just don't know if we can do it."

"I'm sure we can if you help us, Daddy," Deena said. "It would be fun—a sort of family collaboration."

Sam looked at Deena's pleading face, and his expression softened. "All right, Muffin," he said. "If you're game, so am I. I'll be the coach, and you and your friends will be the team. I'll be the ringmaster, and you'll be the circus."

"You'll be Arturo Toscanini, and we'll be the La Scala Orchestra," Deena chimed in enthusiastically. "You'll be Federico Fellini, and we'll be the cast of *La Dolce Vita*. You'll be Ivan Petrovich Pavlov, and we'll be a pack, of experimental—"

"We get the point!" Kathy yelled. Her head was starting to throb. She'd been so hot to save the day for Deena, she hadn't thought about what it would be like to actually *work* with her. She began to wonder if more than thirty seconds of teamwork with her cousin wouldn't drive her right out of her tree. Be calm, she told herself. Stay cool.

"All right," she said out loud. "What we need to do

now is get organized. First, I need to call Mike Iwasaki and the rest of Dementia and ask them to come over here tomorrow morning so I can see if I can talk them into going along with this idea." It was a big *if*, but Kathy didn't say that out loud. Instead she turned to her cousin. "Deena, since you won't actually be performing, you can be in charge of everything else, like decorations and refreshments and costumes."

"Well, of course I'm in charge of all that," Deena said huffily. "I am still the chairperson of the entertainment committee after all, Kathy."

"Speaking of the committee," Sam said, "don't you have to get their O.K. for all this, Deena? I mean, can you two just charge ahead and plan the thing without checking with them?"

"I'll telephone each one of them tonight," Deena said decisively, "and arrange for a meeting first thing Monday morning. If anyone has any objections or suggestions about the idea, we'll just have to deal with them as best we can."

"I don't think they'll give you much lip," Kathy said. "They'll be too relieved to finally hear a normal idea!"

Deena flushed with annoyance, but didn't say anything to Kathy. She couldn't be nasty to her cousin right now, she reminded herself. She was too grateful to Kathy for bailing her out of this mess.

"How's this for a working agenda?" Deena said. "Tomorrow morning I'll run downtown first thing and find as much sheet music and as many tapes from the fifties and sixties as Cranford has to offer. Then I'll meet you two and the band back here at say . . . ten-thirty a.m.?"

"Sounds good to me," said Kathy.

Sam glanced at his watch. "Ten-thirty a.m. it is," he said. He stretched his long legs and got to his feet. "I'll see you ladies down here tomorrow morning. But for now—I'm turning in. I've got some work to do."

Deena and Kathy watched Sam leave the room. Then they turned toward each other and exchanged nervous, shaky smiles. Though they didn't say anything out loud, they knew they were both thinking the same thing. So far, so good. But they had an enormous amount of work ahead of them. And if they could actually pull this thing off, it would go in the record books as a major miracle.

Chapter 10

The next morning at ten twenty-five Kathy sat in the parlor with Mike Iwasaki and the other wild-eyed, long-haired members of Dementia. Every now and then Mike pounded on the side of his fuzzy head as if he were trying to shake pool water out of his ears. "You want *us* to play golden oldies music?" he asked for the seventeenth time. "Like 'Hey, Hey, Paula' or 'Going to the Chapel'?"

Kathy sighed and patiently repeated her explanation for the eigthteenth time. "I know it's not our top pick as performers," she said. "But it *is* a gig—a chance to show what we can do. And besides, I promised my cousin we'd help her out."

Mike got up and came over to face Kathy. "You've been using the word *we* an awful lot in this conversation, Kathy," he said. "It almost sounds like you're thinking of yourself as a permanent member of Dementia."

Kathy stared back at Mike's face in confusion. Then,

suddenly, she knew what she had to do. She wasn't moving back to California anytime in the near future. It was time to put the past behind her and get on with her new life. "I guess you're right!" she said after a long minute. "I guess I am a permanent member of this band now—for better or for worse."

Mike grinned and reached out and shook her hand. "I only hope it doesn't turn out to be for worse," he said. "Less than two weeks to learn all those new—or *old*—songs. I don't see how we can do it."

"We can do it because my uncle's going to help us do it, Mike, and he can do anything!" Kathy said. "He's coming down here to help us at . . . " she glanced at the grandfather clock and frowned. "Well, I guess he's running a little late this morning. But he should be here any minute."

At that instant the parlor door was flung open, and Deena burst into the room. As usual, her arms were filled with folders and papers. "I'm sorry I'm late,"she said breathlessly. "But you simply won't believe how successful I've been. Both the library and the music store stocked more golden oldies music than we'll ever need in this lifetime. I guess it's just as Daddy said yesterday, Kathy. Nostalgia is *in* these days." She put down her papers and looked around the parlor. "By the way, where is Daddy? I want to show him all these things I discovered."

No one in the parlor had an answer, so Deena went out into the hall and called for her mother. "Mom?" she shouted.

Nancy Manelli heard her and came out of the kitchen

88

to answer. "Your mom's upstairs scratching plaster as usual, honey," she said. "Can I help you with something?"

"Well, Daddy's the one I'm really looking for, Aunt Nancy," Deena smiled. "Have you seen him around anywhere?"

Nancy stared at her niece. "Why, yes, Deena, I did see him. Early this morning."

"Well, did he tell you where he was going?"

"Yes, he did, Deena. He . . . " Her voice trailed off and she swallowed hard.

"He *what*, Aunt Nancy? Please tell me where he is. I have a room full of strange but willing musicians in there waiting for him, so I need to find him as soon as possible."

"That's just it, Deena," Nancy said nervously. "You can't find him because he's gone. He left at eight o'clock this morning carrying his suitcase!"

It was at that moment that Deena spotted the large, square white envelope propped up on the hall table. Her name was scrawled across the front. Deena recognized the handwriting at once.

Immediately she snatched up the envelope and charged into the front parlor. "Look at this!" she yelled at Kathy, waving the note under her cousin's nose. "Just look at this and tell me he hasn't done it again!"

Kathy looked completely bewildered. "Wh-what is it, Deena?"

"It's a note from my mean, horrible, *absent* father, that's what it is!"

Kathy reached out for the envelope, but Deena pulled it away. "Well, what does it say, Deena?" asked Kathy. Then her eyes narrowed. "It looks like you haven't even opened it!"

"I don't *need* to open it because I already know what it says. It says that my father had something more important to do this morning than be with his daughter the way he promised. Or with his niece and her band, too, for that matter!"

Crumpling the note into a wad, she marched back toward the door. "Deena, wait!" cried Kathy. "You should read the note. Maybe Uncle Sam had a good reason for leaving. Maybe he'll tell you all about it when he comes back."

"When and *if* he comes back," Deena retorted. "He just *might* try to explain why he left! But it won't do him any good, because I won't be listening—because I am never *ever* speaking to that man again!"

Chapter 11

Two days later a disheartened, still angry Deena sat in front the members of the Spring Fling Entertainment Committee. She didn't waste any time getting started. After her screaming tirade with Kathy in the front parlor on Saturday, she'd stomped upstairs and brooded about her father for the rest of the morning. Both her mother and Nancy had tried to explain her father's reasons for leaving, but Deena was too upset to listen. By the time she rejoined the group, she'd made up her mind. She was washing her hands of her father. She didn't need him. She didn't need anybody—except maybe for Kathy and Dementia. If the group could just get the music to sound decent, they could put on a successful Golden Oldies Spring Fling without any help from Sam at all!

Despite her terrible mood, Deena's committee presentation was worthy of a Madison Avenue power ad campaign. This time, in addition to her papers and folders, she had posters, pictures, and graphs. On the chalkboard she copied a demographic chart from a local radio station, showing how WCRN's listening audience expanded during their "Travelin' Back Through the Years" Golden Oldies Hour of Power. In the background, as she spoke, she played a cassette of Little Richard, screaming a medley of his favorite hits.

At the beginning of Deena's talk, the committee members were showing their usual level of interest in the project. Zack was eating a jelly doughnut, Steve was pushing buttons on his calculator, and Trish was pouting over a chipped nail. Rainier had his usual blank-eyed stare, and Sally was wrapping her knees and ankles with Ace bandages. Only Zee gave Deena her full, critical attention. But, as Deena grimly reminded herself, compared to the kind of attention she got from Zee, a session with a dentist's drill was like a nursery school birthday party.

Nonetheless, approximately forty-five minutes later, when Deena was finally finished with her detailed delivery, everyone but Zee was looking enthusiastic. Even Trish Boswell seemed to have forgotten her beloved Bubble Gums tape and punch concept.

"This is really a fun idea!" she said, leaning forward in her chair. "My mom has a whole collection of old forty-fives she's always playing at home. I just adore some of those corny old tunes."

Trish's enthusiasm made Deena cheer up in spite of everything that had happened. She immediately added several points to her mental estimate of Trish's I.Q.

"Would you mind bringing those records to the inn sometime soon?" she asked her. "The band might need them for research material." The band would need all the help it could get now, she told herself. She thought of the painful, amateurish music Dementia had produced in the front parlor all weekend. The memory sent chills up and down her spine until she shook herself and forced her attention back to Trish.

"I'll go home and get the records right now," the girl was gushing. "I can be back in a jiffy and . . . "

"I can be back in a jiffy," Zee squealed in a perfect imitation of Trish's high voice. "I mean, it's not like I'm not overwhelmed with everybody's enthusiasm and everything, but, like I mean, don't we have to vote on this idea, or something? You yourself said the tunes were corny, Trish. Is 'corny' really where we're at here at Cranford High?"

Deena controlled her annoyance. "I believe Trish was using the adjective *corny* as a term of affection, Zee."

Zee snorted. "Well, knowing Trish, I suppose that's possible. But what about the band then? You said you were coming up with a list of dynamite bands for us to choose from. But like today all I'm hearing is Dementia, Dementia, Dementia. What about all the other bands you were going to come up with? Some vote—with only one band!"

Deena stared at Zee and drummed her fingers on the tabletop. "You know something, Zee?" she said after a minute. "You are truly one of the most negative people I've ever met. You're a regular walking downer, as my cousin would say. You have done nothing but criticize every single thing I've said or done since this committee has started meeting. Now I'll admit my ideas weren't that good. But you certainly never came up with anything better! Not once did you make a single constructive suggestion of your own." She spread out her arms and gestured around the room. "If you have a better idea for the Spring Fling entertainment, by all means let the rest of us hear it!"

For a long moment no one in the room said a thing. To her astonishment Deena thought she actually saw a spark of spirit flash into Rainier Helmutte's lifeless stare, but he quickly turned his face away, so she couldn't be positive. At that moment Zee put both her hands into her armpits and made flapping wing motions. "Gobble, gobble, gobble," she said as she got to her feet. "Welcome to the turkey farm! I knew I should have told the Student Council to take a hike when they begged me to be on this committee. Come to think of it, that's what I *did*. But then the wicked witch of the north, who's also the guidance counselor, told me I had to glom onto some kind of wholesome extracurricular activity, *or else*. But, wow, I mean, like compared to this clueless committee, 'or else' is starting to sound pretty good!"

She picked up her leather jacket with the skull and bones on the back and slung it over her shoulder. "I hope you all have a regular party in here, planning your little dancie-poo," she said as she sauntered out of the room. "I'll see all of you there. I wouldn't miss it for the world."

When Zee had left, Deena sat gazing at the doorway, hardly daring to believe her archenemy was actually gone. Then Trish giggled and Deena snapped back to her senses. "Please accept my apologies for all that," she said brightly. "Let's all try to put it behind us, and move onward and upward. We have a lot to do and very little time in which to do it. So let's begin considering decorations for the gym. Are there any suggestions from the floor?"

A few days ago Deena would have staked her life on the committee responding with their usual bored silence, and she'd been more than ready to supply all the suggestions herself. But today things were different. To Deena's amazement she barely had to open her mouth. Maybe they felt more relaxed without critical Zee in the room, or maybe they just liked the idea of a golden oldies theme. But whatever the reason, the kids were leaning forward in their seats, interrupting each other in their enthusiasm.

"My uncle collects old movie posters," said Steve. "If we promised to be careful, he'd probably let us borrow some to put up around the gym."

"Got an old picture of my pa from 1958, " said Sally. "He's wearing this big letter sweater in it and swallowing a goldfish! Probably could bring it in."

"Old posters and photos are an excellent idea," Deena began, scrawling on her pad. Then she stopped writing and looked at Sally in surprise. "I thought you weren't even coming to the Spring Fling, Sally. What happened to hockey camp?"

"Just decided to go a day late," Sally answered. "This new theme idea makes me want to drop in on the dance after all. Sounds like fun. And I always have liked dressing up in old clothes."

I know precisely what you mean, Deena said to herself,

glancing at Sally's daily outfit of flannel shirt, faded sweat pants, and track shoes. But to be honest, at that moment, Sally's clothes and Sally herself looked radiantly beautiful to Deena. She was so grateful for Sally's support, she felt like kissing one of her ruddy cheeks.

"That's simply wonderful, Sally," Deena said.

"I have the idea!" interrupted Rainier in a heavy, almost unintelligible accent. When he spoke, a collective gasp sounded in the room, and everyone turned to gawk at him. History in the making, Deena thought. The second resurrection! The zombie emerges from its sarcophagus and speaks!

"Why do we not bring in some *live* goldfish to use for the decorations! And what also about a telephone booth? My American parents have been describing to me how they used to crowd as many persons as possible into one, and . . ."

"Very imaginative thinking, Rainier," Deena said. "And I'm sure I speak for the entire committee when I say we're thrilled to hear your ideas. But I think we all need to make an effort to ensure that our suggestions are on a realistic level. Keeping in mind that we have less that two wee—"

"I know!" squealed Trish with a cute little clap of her hands. "We could get some videos from some silly old fifties movies. Maybe we could hook up the school VCR in the gym and play them during the dance."

Deena wrote on her pad again. "I'll make a note to check with the principal about tha—"

"Even better!" Dave cried. "Picture this: we get the old

projector from the AV room and play the movie right on the wall—sort of like a light show, like they used to have in the sixties."

"Oh, what a fabulous idea!" Trish said with another clap. Around the table heads nodded in agreement. From then on Deena gave up trying to control the meeting. It was all she could do to scribble down notes about everyone's wildly flying ideas and who was volunteering to do what. After a while the discussion turned to refreshments, and the same thing happened all over again. The sullen, silent, stagnant committee members had been transformed into excited, enthusiastic, energetic idea machines. And at the mention of food, even the sleepy Zack Rollins came to life.

"Let's have fishbowls full of those goldfish crackers," he suggested. "And maybe even put the punch in goldfish bowls."

"What if we have a big cake in the shape of a motorcycle," Dave put in. "And then we could get all the food servers to dress like greasy hoods in black leather jackets."

"We could serve the cookies in helmets," Zack said. "And sandwiches in hubcaps!"

At this suggestion Deena put down her pen and stared at her committee. She couldn't believe her eyes. Most of the kids were on their feet, shouting and gesticulating to one another across the table. The meeting had turned into a frenzied free-for-all. Things were getting out of control.

"Hold it!" she shrieked. Six yammering mouths snapped shut as everyone turned to look in her direction.

"You're getting carried away," she said more quietly. "Your ideas are wonderful, but we have to find out if they're workable. Now, Trish and Zack: your assignment is to meet with the principal and find out just what our budget is for refreshments." She turned toward Rainier. "You and I will handle decorations. And Steve and Sally will handle all the other miscellaneous items we've mentioned, such as the movies and forty-fives. We also have to think about posters, chaperons, and a lot of other things, so I'll be in touch with all of you over the phone. Call me at home whenever you want. We'll meet here again in three days. Good-by!"

She picked up her papers and folders without dropping a single one and walked out of the room. Behind her, she could hear the kids on the committee beginning to babble excitedly once again. They'd liked the idea better than she'd ever dared to hope. The decorations and refreshments were going to be great. Too bad the music would be so horrendous. With Daddy's help, Kathy and Dementia might have had a fighting chance at learning at least a few good, old songs. But now, left completely on their own, the band was probably going to sound pathetic, and their musical future would be in ruins.

With a long sigh Deena stepped out into the hall. She was just in time to see a bunch of laughing, chattering juniors coming around the far corner. Immediately she recognized Ken, right in the middle of the group. Next to him, practically glued to his side, was the beautiful, red-haired Wendy Blair.

Suddenly Deena had a strong urge to vanish into thin air. She'd barely seen Ken since he'd been back from the government simulation, and she was beginning to think that was the way he wanted it. Every time she'd caught sight of him lately, he'd waved and smiled, and then hurried off to participate in one of his activities. He still hadn't called to ask her to the Spring Fling, and Deena felt more and more certain he wasn't going to. She didn't know what had gone wrong between them, but she did want to hang on to her pride. Right now the last thing she wanted was for Ken to see her standing here alone and pathetic in the middle of the hall while *he* was surrounded by a group of witty, popular upperclassmen.

Desperately Deena glanced around until she spotted the nearest girls' room. As she hurried through the door, she thought she might have heard someone saying her name behind her. Her heart thumped, but then she decided it was just wishful thinking.

"He didn't even see you, Deena," she told her unhappy reflection in the mirror in the bathroom. "*No* one sees you anymore! Ken has just added his name to the list of people who get their kicks by ignoring you."

Her face looked so grim, she decided she'd better fix up her make-up before she went out into the hall again. She reached into her shoulder bag for her lip gloss and found the bag of cosmetics she'd stuffed inside last week. Suddenly she had an inspiration. She'd find a way to *make* people see her! They wouldn't be able to help themselves.

Forty-five minutes later, the new Deena Scott emerged from the girls' room. The hall was empty, so unfortunately, no one was there to get the full effect of the change. No one saw the bright, brassy, almost orange Shimmering Saffron streaks in her blond hair or the vivid green eyeshadow and hot-pink lipstick. No one saw the thick, almost purple layer of color she'd brushed onto her cheekbones. And no one noticed the way her wool skirt had been hitched up six more inches above her knees.

That is, no one noticed until she hit the parking lot. Then almost immediately, Ace Lardner materialized on his motorcycle in front of her. "Hey, Blondie!" he leered. "Is it really you? You look like dynamite!"

Deena looked at Ace's bloodshot eyes and stubby chin and suddenly wondered if her transformation had been such a good idea. Ace was practically *drooling*, for heaven's sake! She'd wanted to get attention, but not *this* kind of attention.

She started to back away from the parking lot and yank down her skirt at the same time. But then she heard something behind her that made her stop short. "Oh, Ken!" a voice was shrieking. "How *do* you come up with these things? You're absolutely the wittiest boy in the state of New Hampshire!"

Deena turned around and saw Ken and Wendy Blair standing by the bike rack only a few yards away. Wendy was still chattering and giggling, but Ken was standing as still as a shocked snowman, staring straight ahead at Deena.

Marvelous, Deena thought. Let him stare. She turned back around to face Ace and swallowed hard. "Does your daily offer of a ride still hold true, Ace?" she asked.

Ace frowned, as if he hadn't quite understood what

she was talking about. Then he figured out what she meant. "You're asking me for a lift, Blondie?" he said in amazement.

Deena was irritated. She didn't want Ken to think she was *begging* Ace for a ride! "Yes, I want a ride," she said through her teeth. "Now do I get one, or what?"

Ace leered again and revved up his engine. "Sure thing babe! Hop on."

Deena took a deep breath and climbed onto the seat behind Ace. As the two of them zoomed out of the parking lot, she forced herself not to turn around and look back at Ken. But that didn't matter anyway. She didn't need to see him. She could feel his eyes burning holes into the middle of her back.

Chapter 12

By the time they neared the inn, Ace was acting like the two of them were engaged. It took all of Deena's powers of persuasion to convince him that all she really wanted was a ride home. She didn't want to go to the dirt bike race at the abandoned James farm. She didn't want to go shoot a few games of pool at Barney's Beanery. She didn't want to join him for a greasy chili-cheese-dog at the bowling alley.

As she and Ace roared up in front of the inn, she realized she was finally going to get her wish for attention—and more. Except for Kathy, almost the entire family was outside with Roy and his crew, inspecting the paint job on the outside of the inn. At the sound of Ace's engine, they all turned around and stared out at the street. When Lydia finally recognized her daughter, the perfect Deena, her mouth dropped open in astonishment.

Deena thanked Ace politely and started to climb off

the motorcycle. He gave her his familiar leer and grabbed hold of her arm. "See you later, babe," he said, yanking her up close to his whiskery face.

"Uh . . . sure, Ace," Deena said. She pulled her arm away as gracefully as she could and started up the front walk. She felt as if she were about to go in front of a firing squad. As she went, the urge to disappear possessed her again, stronger than ever. What had she done? she asked herself. This was all a total, miserable mistake. She'd burned her bridges with Ken forever, and now she was making a spectacle of herself in this absurd get-up in front of the entire family. Not to mention that her mother was clearly ready to hit the roof about the motorcycle ride.

Just then, to make matters worse, Kathy stomped out onto the porch and slammed the door behind her. She started to say something, but then she caught sight of Deena and stopped short. Her dark eyes bugged out of her head as she stared at her cousin's hair, clothes, and make-up.

Without saying a word, Deena marched past everyone and reached out to open the front door. Once inside, her mother put a hand on her shoulder.

"Just a minute, young lady!" she said. "Before you go to your room, you're going to tell me that the scene I just witnessed didn't really happen—that I didn't see my daughter riding around without a helmet on a motorcycle . . . that she wasn't with a boy who is regarded as a public nuisance . . . and that she isn't dressed like . . . like that!"

"I can't tell you that, Mom," Deena said in a choking

voice. "Because it's all true. I was stupid and I'm sorry, but it's all true!"

With hot tears running down her face, she broke away from her mother, climbed the stairs to the bedroom, went into the bathroom, and turned on the shower. Fifteen minutes later she came back out, with all the make-up and at least some of the Shimmering Saffron mousse washed away. She picked up her blow-dryer and started to dry her hair. Then, as she passed the window, she almost dropped the dryer in amazement.

A shiny, bright-red Thunderbird was parked in the front driveway. Her father had come back!

Chapter 13

With her wet hair flying out around her shoulders, Deena ran down the stairs and planted herself six inches away from the front door. She'd forgotten her pledge never to speak to her father again. She was going to speak to him a lot. And right *now*!

Her father came through the door and dropped his suitcase on the floor. When he saw Deena, he held out both his arms for a hug. She put her hands on her hips and glared at him.

"That's some greeting, Muffin," he said with his lazy smile. "I'm almost beginning to get the sense you're mad at me or something."

"Mad at you!" Deena sputtered. "Mad at you! Why . . . why . . . you're lucky I'm even speaking to you at all!"

Sam's smile grew a little forced. "Say," he said. "Let's go into the kitchen and let me whip up one of my famous snacks for both of us. I'm starving." He reached for his suitcase. "And I want to show you the present I got for you on my trip, and—"

"I don't want your stupid present!" Deena cried. "I don't want anything from you, ever again!"

Without another word, Sam put his suitcase back down, took his daughter's arm, and led her into the kitchen. While she yanked back a chair and plopped herself down at the table, he went to the refrigerator and poured two large glasses of apple cider. He carried the drinks back to the table and sat down across from Deena.

He reached out to take one of her hands, but she snatched it away. "All right," Sam said with a rueful shake of his head. "I give up trying to guess. Maybe you better just tell me what's wrong."

"How can you even ask that? After the way you abandoned me and Kathy and the other kids on Saturday? After you said you'd help us and then you just disappeared like that?"

Sam's eyes grew wide with surprise. "But, Muffin," he said. "I left you a note. I explained that my new boss had decided to have a sales training session over the weekend—at the very last minute. He called late Friday night after you were in bed. I didn't have any choice. I had to go."

Deena blinked. A training session for a new job did sound pretty important, she thought guiltily. She stared at her father's earnest face, and her heart started to melt. But then she remembered how angry she was. "Couldn't you have at least waited until I got up so you could tell me in person?" she asked.

"Don't you think you're being just a tad picky about all this, Muffin? I had to go, so I went! I mean, what difference does it make *how* I told you?"

"It makes all the difference in the world!" Deena cried. "I thought you just picked up and left the way you always do! You *knew* how important the dance was to me! You had to know I'd be upset! Why couldn't you at least have called up from wherever you were and told me you were sorry you had to leave? If you actually *were* sorry to leave and weren't really overjoyed at the chance to escape!"

The instant she said the words, Deena wished she could take them back. Sam looked so hurt, she felt as if she'd slapped him right in the face. He avoided her eyes and took a long swallow of his cider. Then he cleared his throat. "I was sorry to leave, Muffin," he said in a low voice. "I'm always sorry. A lot more sorry that you realize."

All at once, as she looked at the real sadness in her father's eyes, Deena's throat felt tight and twisted. She swallowed hard and licked her dry lips. "Then, if it makes you so sorry, why do you always go away, Daddy?" she asked softly. "And why do you hardly ever call or write?"

Sam stared down at his long, strong fingers. He cleared his throat again and started to speak. Then he took another gulp of cider and tried again. "I always mean to call you more, kiddo," he said. "But . . . sometimes it's just so hard for me."

"Hard for you to talk to me?" Deena asked in confusion.

"Yes, hard for me to talk to you. Hard for me to hear your voice, and hear all about what you're doing, and remember how close we were when you were little . . . and yet feel like . . . like now, since the divorce, I can't really be a big part of your life anymore. So that's why sometimes I guess it's just easier for me if I maintain my distance a bit. And I know it's easier for your mother, too."

Deena had never heard her father talk like this. It explained so many things she'd never understood before. As she gazed at him, she felt tears start trickling down the sides of her face. She barely even noticed them. "But, Daddy," she whispered, "that's crazy. You're always a big part of my life—you always will be, whether you're around or not. I just like it better when you're around . . . at least *some* of the time. And as for Mom . . . well, given the way I've behaved today, she'd probably be the first to agree I need a father figure in my life!"

Sam didn't say anything for a long time, but he brushed a hand across his eyes and coughed. Then he looked up at Deena and gave a weak version of his famous smile. "Listen, honey," he said, "I know I've let you down a lot of times in the past. Coming and going. Not calling. Not writing. But you and your mom—you both seem to be doing so well all the time. You're both so good at everything you set your hands to. I wasn't sure you needed me interfering with your life all that much."

This time it was Deena's turn to reach out for her father's hand. "I do need you, Daddy," she said in a choking voice. "I do need you interfering in my life."

Sam took one more drink of cider and smiled again.

108

"You know I can't promise to become a new person overnight, Muffin. I can't transform myself into a stout old hearty but strict Dad with a pipe and a pair of beat-up slippers . . . "

Brushing away her tears, Deena giggled at the image of her tall, handsome dad suddenly changed into a fat, stuffy old father. But Sam was still talking. "But anyway, in spite of that, I feel . . . a lot better about things between you and me. Maybe we haven't—we can't—solve all our problems. But I think we've come a long way toward understanding each other today. And maybe we won't be bashing each other's feelings around quite so much in the future." He squeezed her fingers. "I'm glad we talked about all this stuff, anyway."

"Me too, Daddy. We should have done it a long time ago."

At the same instant they both got up and stumbled around the table to hug each other. They stood in a long, silent embrace. Then Sam stood back and brushed Deena's wet hair away from her face. "Now go dry your mop and get out of that frumpy bathrobe, Muffin," he said. "I'm going to go tell Kathy to get that band of musical weirdos over here, and pronto! We've got a lot of work to do if we're going to get things in shape for that dance of yours."

Chapter 14

The next morning Deena woke up feeling surrounded by a happy, floating glow. As she started off for school, she realized that the success or failure of the Spring Fling just didn't seem that earth-shattering to her anymore. She wouldn't absolutely die if every single detail of the dance wasn't perfect. Of course she was still really excited about the whole thing. But now that she'd had such a terrific conversation with her father, she felt as if she just couldn't get too hysterical and overwrought over something like a school dance.

Still, she was pleased when she ran into Trish Boswell and Steve Rutherford in the hall after school. They told her they'd already rounded up a lot of wonderful decorations and posters for the Spring Fling, and they'd heard the other kids on the committee had some good finds as well.

"Terrific," Deena told them. "Maybe we should have

our next meeting at the inn so we can start storing every-thing there. Pass the word along to the other kids when you see them, O.K.?"

She said good-by to Trish and Steve, then started toward the nearest exit. As she went, she thought about the ups and downs she'd been through in the last two weeks. Life was really amazing, she told herself. You have a problem you think you simply can't solve, and then somehow it works itself out.

Which wasn't to say she didn't still have some problems left to deal with. For one thing, as punishment for the motorcycle ride with Ace, her mother had decreed a two-week grounding to begin the instant the Spring Fling was over. For another, Deena still had a lot of doubts about whether Dementia would be able to learn all those songs before the Spring Fling, even *with* Sam's coaching. And for another, and most upsetting of all, Deena still didn't have a date for the very dance she'd been so busy obsessing about! She'd given up all hope of Ken's asking her—but she'd been so busy dreaming about him for the last two months, she felt as if she didn't even *know* any other boys at Cranford!

Still, she felt better than she had twenty-four hours ago. Maybe Ken hated her now, but at least she knew her father really cared, she thought as she went out onto the parking lot.

Rrrrrrrmmmm! "Hey, Blondie!"

"Uh-oh," Deena said out loud. Apparently, Ace still cared, too! She bit her lip as she watched his motorcycle splash through a puddle and screech to a stop right in front of her.

"Hop on, Toots!" Ace said, patting the seat behind him. "Want to take in the mud wrestling over at the Forum?"

Deena smiled politely. "No thanks, Ace," she said, thinking fast. "I . . . I'm waiting for someone, so if you don't mind, I'll decline your offer."

Ace's face darkened. "But I do mind, Blondie! You can't be my chick one day and then turn off on me the next. Ace Lardner doesn't like that!"

Deena swallowed. She'd always thought Ace was basically harmless, but right now his expression was really angry. His voice sounded like the growl of a mad dog. Why had she ever gotten involved with somebody like this? she asked herself. If he really lost his temper, he could be impossible to handle.

Desperately Deena looked around for help, but the parking lot was completely empty. She was just starting to really panic, when she felt a hand on her arm.

"Sorry I'm late, Deena." Ken's voice in her ear was low and friendly. "Ready to walk home?"

Deena felt like shouting with relief, but instead she simply smiled and nodded. "Sure, Ken. Let's go. Bye, Ace!"

Ace looked like he might argue, but as he stared at Ken's broad shoulders and strong arms, he seemed to change his mind. He muttered something nasty under his breath and then stomped down on his pedal and roared out of the parking lot in the opposite direction. Ken and Deena watched him go in awkward silence. Then, still without saying anything, the two of them started off toward the inn.

After five minutes of plodding along without talking, Deena couldn't stand it anymore. "Listen, Ken," she said miserably. "Thanks for helping me out with Ace back there. But you can leave now. You don't have to *really* walk me home!"

Ken gave her a long, hard look. "You don't want me to walk you home?" he asked. "Did you want to hitch a ride with Ace back there?"

"No! I mean, yes!" Deena stammered in confusion. "I mean yes, I want *you* to walk me home, and no I didn't want to ride with Ace. That was all a big mistake yesterday when you saw me with him, and I...I..." Her voice trailed off in confusion. "I guess I must have looked like a real idiot."

"I thought you looked fantastic," Ken said. "Really sexy. You should wear shorter skirts all the time."

Deena stopped in her tracks and stared at him. "You *liked* the way I looked?"

"Sure. Well, except for the hair, that is. It looks a lot less like a flamingo's feathers today."

All at once they both started laughing out loud. When they were finished, Ken reached out for Deena's hand. "Listen, Deena," he said "Are you mad at me or something? I've been trying to catch up with you since I came back from the capital to ask you to go to the Spring Fling with me, but you've been so busy, I just never got the chance. I tried to call a few times, but your line was constantly busy."

Deena's breath started coming so fast, she thought she might hyperventilate and keel over. "You thought *I* was busy?"

"Well, sure. I mean, I knew you were busy with your Spring Fling committee and everything, but I thought you might have found a *few* minutes to spare for me. Once or twice I even thought you might actually be trying to avoid me!"

Deena's laugh was slightly hysterical. "You thought I was trying to avoid you?" She smiled up at Ken. "Do you think I'm crazy?"

"Well, sometimes, I've wondered..." Ken teased with a laugh. He leaned over and brushed a lock of saffron-tinted hair away from Deena's face. Suddenly he leaned down and grabbed both her shoulders hard. Then he kissed her, right in the middle of the sidewalk.

Chapter 15

The next week and a half was wild and crazy. The preparations for the Spring Fling spread, swelled, and stretched until no corner of the inn was safe from them. Night and day the *beat, beat, thump!* of golden oldies music rocked the foundations of the dignified, quaint old building. The formerly charming front parlor had been completely converted into a rehearsal studio in which Kathy and one or more members of Dementia feverishly practiced whenever they had a chance. Any inn guests who were foolish enough to wander through the parlor door in search of a peaceful place to read *New England Digest* immediately realized their mistake and retreated out into the hall again.

To add to the confusion Deena and her hearty band of committee members were using almost every other available nook and cranny at the inn in which to store the bizarre assortment of paraphernalia they were collecting. These items included Hula-Hoops, saddle shoes, goldfish

115

bowls, hubcaps, soda glasses, Howdy Doody marionettes, Davy Crockett coonskin caps, and an assortment of Elvis posters. As the guests wandered from room to room, searching for a place to sit, they stumbled over piles of outlandish objects and wondered out loud if their relatives had committed them to a mental institution disguised as a country inn.

From time to time Lydia and Nancy made a joint attempt to bring life back to normal at the inn. But their efforts didn't have the slightest impact on what was going on. Deena, Kathy, and the other kids were too deeply submerged in the dance preparations to notice how they were affecting anyone else. The Spring Fling project had become too absorbing, too intense, too gigantic to be ignored. It had taken on a life of its own.

But at last it all ended. The frenzied days and nights of singing, piano and guitar playing, organizing, collecting, arranging, pounding and painting, giggling and bickering, and Big Mac meals on the parlor floor were over. The last note of the last song had been practiced to death. The last elaborate decoration had been hauled to the high school gym and hammered, tacked, or glued into place. Even the refreshments were ready, securely Saran-wrapped onto enormous cardboard platters and arranged on long, folding aluminum tables.

The night of the Spring Fling had finally, *finally* arrived. Deena and Kathy were back at the inn, dressing for the main event, and talking for almost the first time in two weeks.

Deena was sitting at the dressing table, brushing her blond hair into a long, bouncy ponytail. She was wearing a red and white polka-dotted peasant blouse, with the ruffled neckline pulled off the shoulders. Her black spandex pants and ballerina slippers complemented the blouse perfectly. Lydia had found most of the costume right in her own closet. She and Deena had been getting along a lot better in the last few days. Deena had even gone in and volunteered to help with the final coat of varnish for the new reading room floor. Now the project was finally finished, and everyone agreed the upstairs reading room was a beautiful addition to the inn.

Deena was reaching behind her head to tie a hot pink scarf onto her ponytail when Kathy ordered her to turn around.

"What do you think, Deena?" she asked.

Deena's only answer was a gasp and then a shout of laughter. She'd been expecting Kathy to dress like a beatnik or a gang moll or something, but instead she'd gone for a totally teenybopper look instead. She was a completely new person! She was wearing a long, full, black skirt that stood out in a big circle away from her legs. On the front of the skirt was a large pink felt poodle with green rhinestone eyes. The pink of the poodle was a perfect color match for the pink of her fuzzy, round-collared angora sweater.

But the most amazing thing was Kathy's hair. Somewhere she'd dug up a short, teased-up wig that was just like Annette Funicello's hair in the old beach party movies. The wig's color was the same shade as Kathy's own, so it looked like her real hair.

"Way to go, Daddy-o," Deena said. "I particularly love your footwear."

117

"Aren't they radical?" Kathy looked at her scuffed saddle shoes with pride. "I had to hunt all over town for them. Then I had to beat them up with my hairbrush!"

"What's the rest of Dementia going to be wearing?"

"I'm not sure," Kathy said as she bent over in front of the mirror and put on a thick layer of light pink lipstick. "I guess everyone's scrounging up their own stuff at home, just like we did." She straightened up and patted her absurd wig. "There!" she said. "I'm ready. And I think I hear Roy's motorcycle outside, so I'd better push off. He's wearing an Elvis costume tonight, and I can hardly wait to get a load of his rhinestones."

She started out the door, her full skirt swinging out around her. Then she stopped and turned back. "How are you and Ken getting over to the school?"

Deena frowned. "Ken's coming over here any minute in his mother's car. I was hoping Daddy would give us a ride to school in the T-bird, but..." She stopped and gave Kathy a hopeful, worried glance. "I haven't seen him around all day, have you?"

"Well, no I haven't, but..." She came back into the room. "Listen, Deena, don't blow your mind about this. Uncle Sam has been working like a madman to help us get ready for tonight. He said he wouldn't miss the dance for anything. He'll turn up for sure."

Deena twisted her hands together. "I know that's what he *said*, but... where is he then?"

Kathy started to say something when they both heard Roy rev up his engine in the driveway. "Gotta go, Deena! Keep the faith, baby!"

As Deena watched her teenybopper cousin bounce out

118

of the room, she ordered herself not to start worrying about her father. She'd worked hard for tonight, and she wasn't going to let it be spoiled by an anxiety attack now. She turned back to the mirror one last time and tucked a few stray hairs into her shiny ponytail.

As she came downstairs, her mother was letting Ken in the front door. He smiled up at her, and she caught her breath. He looked terrific—but so *different*. Instead of his usual preppie, clean-cut look, tonight he'd dressed himself like a fifties juvenile delinquent, with wraparound black sunglasses, a raggedy T-shirt, black leather jacket, and tight jeans. He'd combed his blond hair back up away from his face, which made him look more handsome than ever. In fact, he looked exactly like a movie star named James Dean whom Deena had seen on T.V. in *Rebel Without a Cause.*

Deena and Ken said hello, and then it was time to go. Lydia and Nancy and even Johnny were all coming by the dance later so they could hear Kathy sing and see Deena's decorations. Everyone waved good-by, and Ken started up his mother's car and took off. As they pulled out of the driveway, Deena took one last look around, hoping to see her father's T-bird speeding toward them. But when the road turned out to be empty in both directions, she decided once and for all that she wouldn't think about Sam for the rest of the evening.

A few minutes later they arrived at the school. Deena and Ken headed straight for the main entrance to the gym. Ken hadn't seen the final decorations, so he was eager to enter, but Deena pulled on his arm, begging him to slow down. She wanted to take her time going in, trying to pretend she was an ordinary mortal, beholding the decorations for the first time. She stood in the doorway for a few minutes. The decorations looked beautiful. Golden oldies memorabilia hung from all the hooks, ladders, folded-up bleachers, wire light cages, and exercise mats in the room. A replica of a telephone booth stood in the center of the floor. Shiny, sparkling goldfish flashed under the lights as they swam in their oversized round glass bowls on the food tables. The place was wild and bright, funky and outrageous.

"This is the cutest dance theme this school has ever had," Trish said, bubbling with excitement. Deena turned to face Trish who was dressed as a Mouseketeer, complete with ears. "Don't you think so, Deena? Don't you think it's just the cutest?"

For once Trish's little-girl squeal didn't grate on Deena's nerves. Tonight it seemed like a perfectly normal way to talk. "I do think so, Trish," she answered. "Yes, I do."

Ken interrupted the conversation to say he was going to get some punch. Then the other kids started arriving at the school in droves, and the Spring Fling was officially underway. Almost immediately, as Deena saw the big crowd of people gathering, she started worrying about the reaction to Dementia. But after the first four mournful "teen angels" of "Teen Angel," she knew she could relax and enjoy herself. The miracle had happened! The band sounded polished, professional, and perfect. Sam's coaching had been magnificent. And Kathy's singing was right out of this world.

Sally Brown and Rainier Helmutte danced right by

Deena's shoulder. "Swell uniforms on the band," Sally barked into Deena's ear. "Where'd you find them?"

Deena stared at her in confusion. Uniforms? She thought Kathy had said the guys on the band were wearing homemade costumes. She looked up at the stage. Sure enough, the unruly, rebellious members of Dementia were outfitted in neat, shiny pink uniforms. Uniforms with the words "Teen Dreamers" embroidered in flowing script on the backs and sleeves. Even Kathy, under her gigantic wig, wore a satin shirt over her pink sweater.

"But how . . . ?"

A voice spoke in her ear. "May I have the pleasure of this dance, miss?" Deena turned around, expecting to see Ken standing behind her. To her surprise, her father was holding out his arms, waiting to dance with her.

"Daddy!" she exclaimed. "I thought you were . . . I thought you'd . . . where on earth have you been?"

"New York City, Muffin. The Big Apple. I drove down there yesterday afternoon and just got back up here an hour or so ago."

"New York City! But *why?*" The band harmonized on a melodious "ooooo," and the answer came to Deena. "The uniforms! Your old Teen Dreamers outfits! You drove all the way to New York just for them?"

"I cannot tell a lie, Muffin," her father said, grinning. "I thought it would be the perfect touch."

Deena couldn't believe her father had made that long trip, just for her. She felt happy tears come into her eyes, and she moved around the gym floor in a fuzzy, joyful

121

daze. After a minute she looked up at Sam. "Don't you have to go onstage and help the band?" she asked.

"Well, to tell you the truth," Sam admitted, "they did beg me to stay up there and hold their hands. But I told them I had to have the first dance with my daughter."

"Thanks," Deena whispered. "For everything."

A few blissful minutes later the song finished, and Sam said good-by for now and headed toward the stage. Ken fought his way through the crowd and took Deena's hands in his. At the same instant Dementia, alias Teen Dreamers, started in on "Rock Around the Clock," and the whole room started bopping to the music.

For the next three hard-rocking songs Deena and Ken danced without stopping, whirling and stomping around the gym, right along with everyone else. While she was moving back and forth across the basketball free-throw line, Deena spotted the bobbing head of every single member of the entertainment committee, including Zee! She was wearing her usual punk outfit—probably as an anti-golden-oldies protest statement, Deena told herself—and appeared to have cut the hair on one side of her head to about one-sixteenth of an inch long. But nonetheless, she seemed to be enjoying herself. As Kathy belted out "Heatwave" from the stage, Zee flailed her arms and gyrated and writhed her body over backwards until her head was six inches from the gym floor.

"I hope she slips a disk and suffers from lower back pain for the rest of her days," Deena began. But when Ken shook his head and shouted that he couldn't hear her over the music, Deena just smiled and shrugged in reply.

If Zee wanted to enjoy the dance that she'd tried to sabotage at every step of the way, Deena would be big about it. A truly magnanimous person was able to forgive and forget. Maybe, someday . . .

"Deena," Ken said in her ear. "The song's over. Everyone else has stopped dancing."

Deena immediately brought both arms to her sides and stood stock-still, glancing around quickly to see if anyone had noticed her jumping around all by herself like that. Fortunately, everyone else's attention seemed to be glued to the stage, where Kathy was making some kind of announcement.

"Yo, party animals!" her cousin was saying. "We have a lot more songs for you tonight, but—" She tried to go on, but she was interrupted by a burst of wild cheering and applause. When the noise had finally stopped, she continued. "But while the band's resting, I want to take time out to thank some people. First, I think we should show our appreciation for the Spring Fling Entertainment Committee, who decorated the gym and made that great food you're all scarfing down out there!"

Again, the gym rocked with clapping and cheering. Kathy raised her hands for quiet. "Second, thanks to my uncle, Sam Scott, who's been working with the band to help us get ready for tonight." More applause as Sam strolled out onto the stage and took a quick bow.

"And last but not least, I want you to thank the person who really made tonight possible. You don't know what she had to go through to make this year's Spring Fling happen, but you can take it from me, it wasn't all a fun fest. So let's hear it for Deena Scott!"

This time Deena thought the gym might actually explode from the blast of noise made by the pounding feet, clapping hands, and screaming voices. She was so stunned by the din that, she stood frozen where she was, staring around her in wild confusion. Finally Ken came to her rescue, taking her by her hand and leading her through the whistling, stomping crowd and up onto the stage. There, Sam and Kathy stood with her in front of the band. They each took one of her hands and raised them in triumph. Then Sam left the stage and let the two girls bask in their glory by themselves.

The clapping and cheering seemed to last for an eternity. While they stood waving and bowing on the stage, Kathy and Deena saw their mothers and Johnny vigorously applauding in the front. The girls exchanged a quick sideways look and grinned at each other.

"Who'd have believed it?" Kathy said under her breath. "You and me . . . "

"I know precisely what you're going to say," Deena said. "You and *I*, the Cranberry Cousins, cooperating members of the same team like this, are an extraordinary phenomenon!"

"Well, that's not *precisely* what I was going to say . . . "

"Sorry. What were you going to say?"

"I was going to say, that you and *me* working together on all this . . . well, it hasn't been half bad!"